I0624350

Chandi
and the
Black Diamond

A Shattered Moon Novel

Suzi Yee

Text Copyright © 2019 by Suzi Yee

Published by Expeditious Retreat Press
Cover by Vivid Covers
Edited by Elizabeth VanZwolle

For information regarding Suzi Yee's novels and to subscribe to her mailing list, see her website at https://www.joseph-browning.com

To follow Suzi on Twitter: https://twitter.com/Joseph_Browning

To follow Suzi on Facebook: https://www.facebook.com/SuziYeeAuthor

To follow Suzi on MeWee: https://mewe.com/i/josephbrowning

By Suzi Yee

SHATTERED MOON NOVELS: CHANDI SERIES
Chandi and the Moonstone
Chandi and the Pearl of Making
Chandi and the Black Diamond

Chapter One

"Chandi, time to wake up," Mika murmured as he gently shook her shoulder. She uttered an unmistakable grumble of displeasure but failed to rouse. Mika marveled at how she managed to claim all the blankets throughout the night but by morning they were cast off in a fit of pique. She always started off the night ice cold, but by the morning, she was as warm as an oven. It was still dark out, but he could appreciate the contours of her body by the sliver of the moonlight coming in through the window. He cradled her from behind and slid his arm around her waist; she instinctively nestled into the curve of his hip. Despite their difference in height, they seemed to fit like two pieces of a puzzle. He rubbed his hand against the soft smooth skin of her abdomen. "Chandi, wake up," he spoke into her ear.

"I don't want to," she mumbled. "It's not even close to morning." She fumbled for the edge of the covers.

"I would love for you to stay in bed with me, but you asked me to wake you so you could get back to your room *before* morning, remember?"

Chandi's groggy head slowly processed his words and her green eyes suddenly opened wide. "Shit—Lucy!"

Mika reclaimed his blankets as she sat up and collected her clothing. She whipped her tousled long black hair into a rough bun while she continued the hunt for her shirt.

"Under the chair," Mika suggested from the bed.

"How did it get there?" she wondered aloud as she crouched down to retrieve it.

"You don't remember? I must be losing my touch," he joked.

Once she was dressed, Chandi sat on the edge of the bed. "Now you're just fishing for compliments." She bent down to kiss him goodbye and lingered a little longer than she intended. His warmth and soft lips pulled her closer to him. She broke the contact before it was too late. "I have to go," she insisted with a huskiness in her voice, "and I don't like to start what I can't finish."

"Sounds like a threat."

"More like a promise." She pecked his cheek. "See you tonight?"

"Sure," he sighed, stroking her cheek before she rose and quietly closed the door behind her. Mika lay back, semi-erect and alone…it was going to be one of those days.

Chandi crept down the dim hallways, familiar with the path from the visiting tracers' quarters to her room. Today was the pathfinder tryouts, and she wanted to be there for Lucy, who was bound to be a bundle of nerves. Halfway there, she nearly collided with her roommate, who was soft stepping from the general direction of Willem's room. They gave each other a nod of recognition before silently proceeding back to their room together.

Chandi waited until the door closed completely before quipping, "You know, we could rent out our room if no one is sleeping here."

"Yeah, but where would we keep our stuff?" Lucy played along. "How's Mika?"

"Still warm and yummy," Chandi answered. "And Willem?"

"Still obsessed with that stupid cube," Lucy scornfully referred to the piece of loot Willem held back from the battlefield last winter, "but I convinced him to put it away." Lucy caught sight of herself in the mirror and grabbed her hairbrush. "Why does my hair always do this when I spend the night? You would think I was running with my hair down in high winds."

"At least you can attribute some of it to your curls," Chandi commiserated as she let down her hair. "I have bone-straight hair and it's like this every time." She worked the tangles with her comb.

"Do think its deliberate? Like they don't stop until your hair is a mess?" Lucy speculated.

"I don't think there is that much thinking going on," Chandi countered. Both laughed at the expense of their paramours.

"Are you nervous?" Chandi changed the subject.

"A little, but I managed to get some sleep last night." It was one of the things Lucy liked about Willem—he had a way of calming her down when she was keyed up. She was used to taking care of everyone else; it was nice to have a sanctuary when things got too much. She ran into the same mat of hair for a third time. "Stupid knot!"

"You're going to have a bald spot if you keep pulling," Chandi chided. She grabbed the brush and started at the ends, working her way up to the scalp. "You're going to do great… you've got this." She handed back the brush to Lucy.

"That's what I keep telling myself," Lucy muttered under her breath as she started weaving her auburn locks into a tight braid.

They finished their morning ablutions before walking through the courtyard to the main hall for morning devotion. The predawn air still had a crisp chill, but the morning dew would be gone by noon, and the first blush of budding flowers meant that spring had arrived. The pile of rocks had been cleared, and the breech in the wall was encased in wooden scaffolding while the last of the repairs were underway.

Morning devotion was abuzz with the ambient energy radiating from the novices who were testing today. There were as many entrants this time as there were the last time, again forcing the pathfinders and tracers-in-training to run the ruins this morning as the adaptive training grounds, instructors, and support staff would be occupied until lunch. It had been almost a year since Willem and Chandi had become pathfinders, and all they could do was wish Lucy and Hanu well before leaving for training.

*****

Dora, Aka, Zera, and Sabin stood side-by-side waiting for the pathfinders-in-training just inside the gates. "I'm not so sure this is a good idea," Zera wavered.

"It's a little late for doubts," Sabin commented. "You seemed fine with it during planning."

"Well, that was when they were just ideas on paper." She hesitated before speaking, "What if someone gets hurt? That will be on our heads."

"If someone gets hurt, we take them to the infirmary," Aka answered matter-of-factly.

"What if the challenges are too hard?" Zera spitballed.

"Zera, we've spent the past three months training them. We deliberately selected obstacles that would challenge our trainees' weak spots. If they aren't ready by now, everyone needs to know. Coddling them will not better serve them," Dora spoke with care. "Their training is almost over and it would be worse to send them out into the ruins as pathfinders without knowing for certain if they're ready."

Zera squared her shoulders. "You're right. It's going to be fine. We'll keep an eye on them, but eventually they have to sink or swim." Dora smirked at her analogy; of amphibious stock, Dora came into the world swimming.

"For future reference, you should voice your concerns before we spend all morning placing flags around Watertown," Sabin snidely remarked. Dora snorted and Aka grinned, but Zera had already reset her game face and kept her steely gaze fixed to the gates.

As the pathfinder trainees trickled in, Zera called them to attention and explained the exercise. "We have placed a number of flags throughout Watertown. Your objective is to collect as many as possible in the next four hours and return to the gate. You will run as a sept but each pathfinder should hold on to the flags that they personally collect. We will be following your progress along the way."

It took them a moment to comprehend what was happening. This was the first time they were tasked to move as a sept without being led by an instructor. There was some discussion about who should lead. As the oldest trainee, the mantle eventually fell to Willem. When it came to routing and strategy, it was a more contentious discussion. Acutely aware that the clock was ticking, they came to a decision: run out and make a counter-clockwise perimeter sweep around the monastery with periodic radial bursts to widen the search if they don't see any flags en route. "Signal when you see one and you get first stab at retrieval. If you fail, everyone else gets a shot," Willem proposed to group consensus. This is why they chose him as sept leader—he was sensible, fair, and direct. With the rules of the sept established, the eight pathfinders took off, their trainers not too far behind.

They traveled in diamond formation with Willem in the front and the others trading slots as they flowed over the ruins. It wasn't long before Joshi called out, spotting the first flag. It fluttered thirty feet in the air off a rafter. Willem raised his hand, signaling the sept to pause. Joshi ran headlong at a nearby beam, using its trajectory to give him height before he pushed off and propelled himself into the air, five feet short of the flag. He landed hard but his supple hips and knees cushioned the impact, even if there was little to soften his disappointment. Willem opened it up the others. Jukka tried the same approach as Joshi, only he slung out one of his thorny vines from his arm at the apex of his leap, just missing the tip of the flag. Finn tried a series of smaller vertical jumps but couldn't manage to get close enough to grab the flag. Mira, Natalie, and Chandi each tried tic-tacking different corners, hoping to reach some part of the girder and walk their way over to the flag—sadly without success.

Then Yan did something most peculiar. She tic-tacked up a different section, cat pulled herself on top of the wall, made a series of small horizontal and vertical jumps leading her higher and higher into the air, and dropped *down* to the beam, grabbing the flag and tucking it into her pocket before rolling through the drop to the ground. As the sept moved on, Zera beamed with pride that one of hers spotted the first flag and the other claimed it.

*****

Lunch was a tense affair. Lucy and Hanu were tight lipped about the pathfinder tryouts and no one wanted to bring it up—they would know soon enough come dinnertime. Willem and Chandi were battered and bruised from training. All told, the sept collected ten flags and Willem and Chandi each had two flags under their belts; like the first, each had been hard won. As Willem and Chandi filled the quiet with details from the morning's meditations, Sura politely nodded and wondered who she was going to dine with when they all left her.

As they dispersed for their afternoon activities, Chandi quickened her steps to catch up with Willem. "So…" Chandi nudged him.

"So what?" Willem muttered back.

Chandi rolled her eyes. "How do you think it went?"

"You were with me all morning; how should I know?" he answered defensively.

"Did they seem cagey to you?" she speculated.

"I'm not even sure what that means," he replied dismissively.

"You know, secretive…cautious"

"Chandi, I *know* what 'cagey' means. I mean, I don't have any more insight into how Lucy or Hanu might have done in their tryout than you do."

Chandi crinkled her nose; if Lucy were here, she would have totally got it. She was contemplating why Willem was so touchy until it suddenly dawned on her.

"You're worried about Lucy." It was more a statement than a question.

Willem sighed. "It really tore her up last time. I don't want to see her go through that again."

"She's tougher than you give her credit," she commented.

"Maybe I'm not tough enough to watch her hurt like that," he mumbled. Chandi saw genuine anguish pass over his face before he pushed it away.

"You will be, if she needs you to," Chandi reassured him. He nodded and she changed the subject to territory that was less sensitive.

"Have you cracked the cube yet?" she needled Willem, knowing full well the answer was "no."

Willem's face soured. "Lucy shouldn't have told you. I could get in a lot of trouble if anyone found out."

"Did Lucy tell you about my pearl?" she asked pointedly.

"Yes," he reluctantly admitted. Chandi's gave him an oblique look.

"Have you let Lucy take a crack at it? She's pretty good at puzzles," Chandi suggested.

It was Willem's turn to shoot Chandi a knowing glance. "You think she could have gone three months without giving it a go?"

Chandi let out a short laugh. "Well, maybe I'll have better luck, if you're okay with that."

Willem cleared his throat as they neared the classroom. Chandi took the hint and switched to safer topics. "We sorta kicked ass this morning, didn't we?"

"We didn't do too bad, no." Willem's modesty was undercut by the swagger in his step. They entered the classroom for Applied Tenets of Faith, taught this afternoon by the tracers-in-training with an assist from a few visiting tracers. Chandi gave an almost imperceptible nod in Mika's direction as she took her seat on the mats.

After the direct attack on the monastery, Applied Tenets of Faith had taken a slightly different direction. The general principle was the same: turn your attacker's energy against them, but more focus was placed on disarming opponents and how to break a grapple. It followed that in order to practice these defensive skills, the pathfinders needed to be taught how to attack. So the past three months had been about using the flow of energy to flip, trip, topple, and pin your opponent. As they took turns attacking each other, both their attack and defensive skills sharpened.

Aka's hulking form stood in front of the room, reviewing techniques and principles that allowed smaller, weaker opponents to win in physical contests. The trick was to wait for the stronger opponent to exert energy, which could then be used against them. To illustrate his point, he had Mika try to attack him without much success. However, when Aka became the aggressor, the tracer was able to loop and sweep Aka's standing foot out from under him in mid-stride and knock him to the ground. From there, Mika wrapped his legs around Aka's neck and torso and held on for dear life until Aka signaled an end to the demonstration. As they paired up on the mats, Mira whispered to Natalie, "I'd wrap my legs around that." A sly knowing smile tickled the corners of Chandi's mouth. Aka might be seven feet of tattooed muscle, but that was nothing against a determined Mira.

Chapter Two

Ryland stepped back and eyed his handiwork. The abbess was more than pleased to hear that the plasma gun was still operational, but the targeting system had been completely destroyed when the wall came down. It took Ryland the better part of a month to find the right parts between Bartholomew's junk pile and Watertown's ruins, but it was done. The tinker called out an alert below before switching the system on. The red lights turned green and Ryland put it in test mode. He hurled a large rock from the scaffolding and a searing beam of plasma cleaved it in half. *That's fixed in anyone's book.* He patted himself on the back and switched the gun to sentry mode.

He absorbed the tool into his palm and wiped the grime off his hands with a rag before donning his gloves. From his high perch, he looked out over the monastery. Beyond that, rising into the air past the far wall, the ruins of Watertown loomed. The novices were trying out to become pathfinders. The pathfinders-in-training were completing the circuit they'd started shortly after breakfast. The Order of the Guard were making their way back from patrolling the ruins. The trees in the orchard were sprouting new foliage, and rows of little green shoots dotted the gardens, soaking in the sun. He rubbed the day-old growth on his chin—Jackson had finally convinced him to shave, but Bibi liked a little stubble. There were worse places to be; founders knew he'd run all over.

He climbed down the latticework of wood and metal and made his way to the guards' commissary for lunch; Jackson should be back by the time he got there. The tinker-runner had not anticipated how much pleasure he got out of having lunch with an old friend. They had done most of the catching up they felt they needed to do and now they were just hanging out, like when they were young and had nothing better to do. There was something satisfying about being with sentients that knew you when you were young; you had history and context, someone who remembered how you used to be and not just how you were now.

"Catch anything good?" Ryland greeted the sorcerer as he peeled off from the soldiers.

"Blissfully quiet," Jackson replied, gripping Ryland's gloved hand in greeting.

"Then why the long face? Don't tell me you miss the hubbub." They went inside for their stew and brew.

"No, but I just can't shake the feeling that something is wrong. Or not right..." Jackson grasped ineffectually for the precise words. It was a niggling notion that hadn't left him since the night of the wastelander attack. As far as he could tell, it wasn't otherworldly, although the eternal the wasteland sorcerer summoned was about as wrong as you could get. At first, he blamed the x-ray Ryland had conducted, but Chandi came to visit and reassured him she wasn't the least bit nauseated near him, and any trace radiation that might have lingered should have been purified in her near-proximity. Then he thought it might have been increased exposure to tech via Ryland, but he knew that Ry kept his nanites at bay when they hung out and had slowly become accustomed to his presence at the monastery.

"Are you sure you aren't just being paranoid?" Ryland suggested as kindly as he could.

"It's possible, but my gut hasn't let me down yet, so it seems like a bad idea to start questioning it now," Jackson reasoned. "And just because you're paranoid doesn't mean they aren't coming for you."

Ryland chuckled and handed him the salt, just in case he wanted to throw some over his shoulder. "Could it be all the repairs that are going on around the monastery? Most of it is low-tech, but not all. Maybe you're picking up on ambient tech."

"Could be," Jackson replied, unconvinced. "But enough about my delusions…you have news."

Ryland raised an eyebrow. "What makes you think I have news?"

"You're meeting me for lunch out here instead of in the

monastery, for a start," Jackson pointed out.

"Maybe I just wanted a beer," Ryland intoned innocently.

"You're welcome to another—I'm buying," Jackson joked, as the beer was free. "So out with it."

Ryland lowered his voice and leaned in. "I've been offered a position at Unseen Waters."

"Really?! What kind of position?"

"Part teaching, part tech."

Jackson grinned. "The abbess got used to having a tinker on-site?"

"I know how to make myself useful…"

"No doubt. So what does this mean for your other roles in the church?" Jackson skirted delicately around the issue.

"That's the sticking point. If I take the position, I think my tracer days may be over," Ryland rubbed the rim of his empty mug with his thumbs.

"Is that such a bad thing?" Jackson posed the question.

Ryland looked up from his cup. "Why do you ask that?"

Jackson shifted in his seat. "I'm not saying you're old, because we're about the same age and I'm sure as hell not old, but you've been doing this a long time, even discounting the years you weren't with the church…ever since you were seventeen. Wouldn't it be nice to stop traveling all the time? Have a place to put your stuff that isn't a backpack? You took an oath to go where you were needed, and maybe this is where you are needed next."

Doubt crept over Ryland's countenance. "Can you really see me as a teacher?"

"Look, I'm no good with kids, but I have been told that you can be a charismatic communicator when you want to be. And they aren't all kids. The pathfinders and tracers-in-training need preceptors and advisors. That's more one-on-one, and I think you'd be great there. You definitely understand the oppositional defiant mind." Jackson took a long drink as Ryland threw him a stink eye.

"Why do I feel like I've been insulted?"

Jackson shrugged. "Don't know, maybe you're paranoid."

*****

The tension of lunch broke come dinnertime as the dining room filled with chatter about the posted results from the pathfinder tryouts. Lucy beamed throughout the meal, pleased to see the glorious four-letter word next to her name: pass. She tried to hold back her excitement out of respect for Hanu, who had failed, but once he assured them that he was fine, the floodgates of celebratory relief opened. Sura was happy for Lucy, and she told herself that she would have swallowed her disappointment and been happy for Hanu had he passed, but she couldn't deny how relieved she was that he would still be there to train with her.

It was a temperate night, and Willem suggested a nighttime

stroll to celebrate. Lucy found it sweetly romantic but had something she needed to do first. She grabbed a light jacket and hunted down Hanu in the orchard, sitting alone in one of the trees. He scooted over as she climbed up.

"What did you do?" Lucy quizzed him pointedly.

"What are you talking about?" Hanu brushed her accusatory tone aside.

"Last year, you were one minor injury away from passing and this year you failed," Lucy paused, building her case. "And when we saw the results, you didn't look the least bit surprised. So I'll ask you again, what did you do?"

Hanu stared out at the rows of trees. "Nothing you wouldn't have done if you were in my position."

"Hanu, this is serious! If they find out that you are deliberately not progressing at your own pace, they could throw you out," Lucy whispered in case anyone else was close enough to hear.

"Which is why I tried out, took my sweet time during the test, and only grabbed five flags. Anyone could chalk up my performance as an overcorrection from my injury at the last tryouts," Hanu calmly responded. He could feel the weight of Lucy's stare bearing down on him. "They let Willem stay a novice until eighteen and test four times. I'm only turning sixteen in two months, and my tryout fits a perfectly acceptable narrative. I'll be fine, you'll be fine, and Sura will be fine."

"You really like her, don't you," Lucy lowered her judgment

a few notches.

"She's not like you and Chandi, or even Willem. She's not a believer, she doesn't love running, and she didn't come here because it was an opportunity for something better. She's here because she doesn't have anywhere else to go. She's gotta make it out of here as a runner, and that's not going to happen if we all abandon her."

Lucy touched his arm lightly. "Hanu, as long as I've known you, getting out of here has been your top priority."

"And I will, eventually. But not without Sura," he stated resolutely. Lucy put her arms around him and squeezed; she didn't know what else to do. Lucy was about to climb down when Hanu stopped her. "Don't let anyone else know, for real. I don't want Sura to find out. I don't want her to feel bad for something that was my decision."

Lucy looked up at her simian friend. "When did you become so grown up?"

An impish grin spread across his face. "Don't tell anyone…I have a reputation to uphold."

*****

Chandi knocked on the stout wooden door and waited until Brother Bartholomew bade her to enter. The scholar was at his table, making a few observations on outstanding experiments before calling it a night. "Chandi! Take a seat and make yourself comfortable. I'm almost finished." The pathfinder anxiously browsed the stack of books along the far wall, trying to find a tome she hadn't read.

Chandi didn't know where to go or who to tell after her pearl of making glowed in her hand during Longest Night. It didn't shine nearly as bright as Moonstone, but the similarities were too astounding to ignore. The only problem was that she hadn't gotten it to glow since. She even tried holding her freshwater pearl in the moonlight, although all she got was soaking wet. While she was fairly sure that she didn't imagine it, she couldn't be a hundred percent certain positive—she *had* stayed up all night in ritual or tending to the wounded. Without being able to reproduce it, it was her word against the pearl's.

When she came to Brother Bartholomew for help, the scholar offered to run additional tests using the newly refurbished equipment Ryland was rapidly repairing from the pile in the basement, but each test failed to shed new light on her dilemma. Was the core of her pearl of making a piece of Moonstone? Was Moonstone somehow a part of its manufacturing process? Or had Chandi hallucinated the whole thing?

The last thing that Brother Bartholomew could think of was to try an acid bath. If it worked, it would destroy the pearl, but it would reveal the bead at its center. Chandi reluctantly agreed, which was why she was here tonight…to see once and for all if a piece of Moonstone lay in the heart of her pearl of making.

Brother Bartholomew had kept a close watch on Chandi these past few months, looking for signs of disturbance or the melancholy that plagued her when she was Moonstone's brief keeper. He had helped her draft her request for continuation of service to the church, and he made excuses to keep her coming by every so often so he could get the gestalt of her wellbeing. To his observant eye, if it was Moonstone, it wasn't affecting her the same way as before. She was doing well in her training and was generally cheerful, although it didn't take a scholar to figure out a certain tracer who frequently came back to Unseen Waters between assignments had some bearing on her buoyant mood.

He studied her profile, sitting quietly and reading in one of his chairs. He wasn't sure if it was good news or bad, but hopefully it would give her some peace of mind. The owl gathered the newly cleaned pearl and placed it into her hands. "I'm sorry, my dear, but the acid bath didn't work. I took the pH down to 2.4 to no avail. It's just vinegar but I have rinsed it thoroughly, mostly to remove the smell and stop it from flavoring any water produced from it." Bartholomew's bushy eyebrows fluttered at the thought of drinking vinegar water. "I believe the nanite-infused nacre makes it more resistant or less porous than a regular pearl, and if it is a byproduct of tech, I don't know a way to remove that from an object short of breaking it altogether."

Chandi rolled the pristine gray pearl in her hand. "So where do we go from here?"

"Short of smashing it under a heavy rock, there's not much to do, but I'm not entirely sold that you have to do anything more." Bartholomew took a seat opposite her and lit his pipe. "You came to me with your concerns, and we've thoroughly investigated them. We haven't been able to prove or disprove that your pearl of making has any concrete connection to Moonstone. That said, there are no more reports of increased spirit activity, so the danger of Moonstone has been neutralized, one way or another. Maybe you can just enjoy a nice gift from a thankful patient you helped."

Chandi listened to her mentor and took his words to heart, but her conscious was still unsettled. "But what about my dreams? What if Moonstone is in trouble...in pain? Imprisoned? What if it's asking me for help because I'm the only one it can reach? Isn't it my responsibility to do something?"

Bartholomew sat back and considered the implications of her words. "I think there are a few key concepts we must address individually. Let's look at the timeline. You didn't even have the pearl of making when you first had a dream that reminded you of Moonstone, correct?" Chandi nodded. "And you haven't had any other dreams in the past three months?" She confirmed his understanding. "Then, it is entirely possible that Moonstone caused your pearl to glow momentarily without it being physically nearby; that it has sought you out even though you are no longer physically carrying it."

After a few puffs of his pipe, he continued, "Regardless, I do not believe that implicitly makes you responsible for whatever predicament in which it currently finds itself. When you were Moonstone's keeper, it was for the sake and safety of your brothers and sisters of the stride; you were there to *limit* its effect under the shattered moon until a more effective solution presented itself."

The owl shifted in his seat and rephrased her conundrum. "You have a connection with Moonstone, but does that necessitate a responsibility to it?" Chandi knew from years of tutoring that it wasn't a question she was supposed to answer; Bartholomew was fond of the Socratic Method to stimulate thought.

"If Moonstone reaches out to you again, I would advise caution—even the most reasonable sounding desires can lead to disastrous effects. If you pursue a closer understanding of Moonstone, you must be able to separate your empathy from your analytical reasoning, a tall order for any sentient, but especially difficult for someone who uses her innate abilities to heal."

"So, don't let Moonstone use my good nature against me?" Chandi paraphrased.

Bartholomew answered her with another question, "Don't you think those wastelanders out there were in pain and asking for help when the tide turned against them?"

Chapter Three

His Tentacled Majesty Halldix Kepoi sat in his chambers surrounded by an entourage of advisors, all vying for his attention. Each day brought a series of problems, complaints, and requests that demanded his royal attention. Even after all business had been completed, he still had social obligations that came with wearing the girdle of power: luncheons, teas, cocktails, dinners, parties, dances, festivals, and concerts. He had only been king regent for a little over two months, but his entire life had become consumed by the bejeweled belt fastened under his visceral hump.

His uncle's mating ritual took place shortly upon his return from Oswego. Droxithal Purammon would have preferred a more private affair, but his station demanded an audience, and Halldix's penultimate act of filial duty was to make sure it was tasteful. The royal pool was filled with fresh water, lit by the soft glow of bioluminescent plants. Representatives of all six noble families were given seats, each allowed to choose a female among their house to receive his seed. His Tentacled Majesty rose up on his legs, undulating his prominent suckers and grinding his disks in a powerful display. The female octopoids pantomimed according to tradition, feigning disinterest only to be wooed by his show of virility. One by one, each receptive female stood tall as Droxithal approached and slipped his hectocotylus into her mantle cavity, depositing his sperm packet within. The spectators would shift the colors under their skin, counting how long Droxithal spent inside her before she retreated, dragging him along until he retracted.

Once the pageantry was completed and his uncle spent, Halldix began Droxithal's funerary arrangements—his senescence would not be long after mating. The same would be true of the six honored females once they laid their fertilized eggs, but their death rites were their families' concern, not Halldix's. Keeping with tradition, the mortal remains of His Tentacled Majesty Droxithal Purammon, son of Kronar, were chopped into pieces and sprinkled into the royal pool to nourish his offspring. The temperature and circulation of water would be closely watched as Droxithal's brood gestated, and so the Lordship of Fingers observed another cycle of life and death.

From there, it was a whirlwind of activity. In his dwindling weeks, his uncle had become lax in his duties. Essential tasks that were already delegated continued, but other matters were left unresolved. Halldix considered relocating his lab from Rochester to Syracuse in the vain hope that he could continue his tinkering once the initial backload was cleared, but the reality of court life soon corrected him. After his coronation, Halldix was under constant scrutiny; as soon as a brief moment of quiet arrived, a wave of nobles or one of his five advisors descended upon him. Things never slowed down, only shifted laterally. He had so few precious moments to himself, that he simply enjoyed the silence and went through the motions of tinkering, letting the familiar vibrations of his nanites sooth him. His inspiration, his sense of discovery, his zeal for life eked out under a mountain of duty.

Perhaps he needed to get away. Droxithal's brood had hatched and were growing at a prodigious rate. There was an army of minders and tutors to see them through. The king regent considered visiting his old stomping grounds in Rochester but found the notion of moving deeper into octopoid territory unappealing.

One of his advisors flashed a bright patch of yellow, catching his wandering attention. Halldix noted the weighty silence in the room—they were waiting for a reply to an unheard quandary. "Your Tentacled Majesty, how would you like me to proceed in regards to the reports of spirit activity in Oswego?" Vissix skillfully prompted her lord, while maintaining the dignity of his position.

Halldix raised himself in his seat. "Send a message to the Church of Parkour. They deftly handled the spirit problem last autumn and warned that it may be recurring." He sensed mixed reactions among his entourage; not all were keen on his permissive use of vertebrates. "Should they agree, I will greet them as I did before."

His announcement elicited a flurry of color and Yakim, ever the conciliatory peacemaker, stepped forward. "Do you feel that would be wise with the elevation of your status, Your Tentacled Majesty?"

Halldix felt his three hearts beat true at the idea of the frontier. "Make appropriate arrangements for travel." With that proclamation, he sent waves of iridescent flickers across his body signaling his advisors to leave. Immediately.

*****

Mika brushed Chandi's hair aside and nuzzled the soft curve of her neck, placing a trail of kisses down her clavicle, but he perceived a discernable lack of response—no giggles or moans, no playful banter, no leaning in or pulling away. He came up and found her staring with a faraway look in her eyes. "We don't have to do this if you aren't feeling it tonight."

Chandi blinked back to reality. "Sorry, I'm just a little distracted." She shook out her body and relaxed. "Totally ready for sexy, fun time."

"First, you don't have to apologize." Mika sat up and propped himself against the wall. "And second, I'm pretty sure it doesn't work that way, but you get credit for the sentiment." He motioned her to join him. "Why don't you just tell me what's wrong?"

"Why does something have to be wrong?" she asked defensively.

"Because you've never unresponsive to that," Mika bluntly answered. Chandi was about to object until she realized it was true. She sat up and leaned against him, but not before elbowing him lightly in the ribs. She remained quiet, taking comfort against Mika's chest.

"Is it something to do with training?" Mika nudged her.

"No, I'm actually pretty excited to start tracer training." She ran her fingers along his three chest hairs.

He bent his head down. "Something with Lucy?"

"No, we're cool, although pathfinder training is definitely putting her through her paces."

He wrapped his arms around her and kissed the top of her head. "I'd like to help if you'll let me." Mika waited and held her—he could be patient when he needed to be. He felt the tension in her shoulders and back release with time.

"I got my dates approved to visit my family," Chandi eventually spoke. Mike knew it was a stipulation she'd found hard to obtain, but from her tone, he gathered all was not well.

"This was something you really wanted a few months ago. Has something changed?"

"No. Yes. Maybe?" Chandi uncharacteristically wavered. She generally knew which side her bread was buttered on and uncertainty didn't suit her. She felt so silly.

"If you want me to understand, you're going to have to use more words," Mika told her.

"When I thought about seeing my family again, I imagined this great reunion. My parents were going to recognize me immediately, even though it's been twelve years, and my sister and I were going to discover some quirk that we both have even though we've never met. There was going to be a lot of happy crying and hugging. But now that I have a date, it's suddenly real." Chandi paused. "What if it's just really awkward or we don't get along? What if me going spoils everything?" She waited for Mika's response, but it took him some time to gather his thoughts.

"I'm not the best person to help you with family stuff," he admitted. "I haven't seen mine since I joined the church. But I do know that no good comes from unrealistic expectations. It's nice to have dreams and hopes about what could be, but it's not really fair to make someone live up to an idealized image of them in your head. Not for them or you. Real life is messy, even when it's good."

"Why didn't you ever go back to see your family after you became a tracer?" she probed. She felt Mika's body tense beneath her.

"You had loving parents who enrolled you into church service to give you a better opportunity. Not everyone's parents had such noble intentions, and some relationships are better left in the past." Mike failed to hide his lingering bitterness.

"I didn't mean to pry," she apologized.

Mika softly laughed into her hair. "Yes, you did. You give Lucy a hard time about being nosy, but you are just as bad, only quieter about it."

"You may have a point," Chandi accepted his observation begrudgingly. "What I meant was I didn't mean to bring up things that were going to cause you pain."

He hugged her. "I know. And I appreciate that, but that doesn't really help you."

Chandi exhaled. "No, I heard you. Stop being a dumbass and putting them on a pedestal from which they are most certainly going to fall. If I'm going to meet them, I just have to let it be what it is and see if that's something I want."

Chandi never failed to astound him—it took him years to make peace with his family situation, and it took her less than five minutes. By her tone and manner, she might as well have said something obviously basic, like, "It's Tuesday."

Mika chuckled and kissed the top of her head. "Let's get some sleep. Things may look less bleak in the morning, and if you still have reservations, you don't have to visit them just because you can." He blew out the candle and lay back in bed. She snuggled against him and he put his arm around her waist. Together, they found the stillness in the night.

*****

Dora came to the surface, chilled by the breeze coming off the lake. The drysuit made the frigid water bearable while she was fully submerged, but the promise of dry clothes and a warm fire was enough to entice her out of Lake Ontario. She toweled herself off and retreated to her tent before shedding the dive suit and bundling up. The glimmer of honest sunlight was a cold comfort as the wind picked up by the water.

She huddled by the fire, taking a warm bowl from the communal pot. Amphibious sentients were not fond of cold as a general rule, and Dora hoped the heat from the fire and stew would quicken the process. She had been diving for five days, told only to look for a rock painted in the UV spectrum. It was an odd assignment, but it was a small inconvenience if it meant expediting her tracer training. Her time spent running as a pathfinder taught her that sometimes, it was better not to ask questions, especially when the request came from the elder council.

She had swum out farther and farther each day, and today she had finally found something: small pebbles with one side that radiated in the UV spectrum. It wasn't nearly the size Sister Cassandra described, but Dora collected them on a hunch— naturally occurring bioluminescent flora would coat the entire exposed area, not just one side of a pebble. Sufficiently warmed, Dora grabbed another blanket and leaned up against a tree to watch the sunset over the water. Streaks of blue, pink, and orange painted the sky, echoing back onto the lake. It might be colder than she liked, but it felt good to be back in the water. She rose and methodically traced the letters on the tree that drew her eye: RS + CC. She wondered who they were, what brought them to the lake, and how long ago they'd etched their initials into the tree. She shuffled the handful of pebbles in her pocket and approached the sorcerer's tent.

"This is it?" Cassie stared at the four small rocks on her desk, not much larger than pieces of gravel. The sorcerer donned gloves before examining them under the UV light. The intermittent pink glow was unmistakable. "Where did you find them?"

"I swam westward along the shore, maybe ten miles out," Dora answered succinctly.

"Ten miles out and back? That's an incredible distance to cover in a day," Cassie commented.

"I was swimming long before I could run."

"Of course," Cassie replied without much thought. "That will be all." Cassie dismissed her with a curt nod and leaned back in her chair. On the whole, things had pretty much gone according to plan. The spirit bomb started to release spirits during an unseasonable warm spell, and the octopoids contacted the church for support. Cassie combed the woods for the tree Ryland carved his and Chandi's initials into and diffused the ball of wax and salt—she knew the nastier spirits she'd put in its core. Sure, she could have fought them again and it would have been easier the second time around, but she would prefer not to. With all the lunar spirits safely stashed into the pendent, the sorcerer proceeded to put on a good show, making expeditions into the ruins to provide cover to the diver she'd recruited out of Unseen Waters—the UV light wouldn't work underwater, so she had to use a sentient who could do it the old fashioned way.

Cassie closed her eyes and listened intently. If this was all that was left of Moonstone, it wasn't enough to stir the otherworld of its typical chatter. She sighed and chalked it up as a partial win; her intent of finding Moonstone was to mine it for unique spirits. At least she could report a technical mission success to the elder council. As a precaution, she placed the four pieces of rock in the containment box; the otherworld was rarely as cut and dry as sentients hoped.

Cassie prepared herself for dinner with His Tentacled Majesty. She was surprised to find Halldix at Oswego when she arrived a little over a week ago. The months since they'd last met hadn't been kind to him, and she didn't think it had much to do with the poisoning she'd orchestrated last fall. He looked haggard, and the curious lightness of being had left him. She brought her notes from Ryland's experience with sentients of octopus lineage and applied them during their dinners. She started distinguishing facial expressions and picking up on social cues more readily.

Her first observation was that for a race that dies shortly after mating, octopoids are ridiculous flirts. After a few days by the lake, Halldix found his humor and a measure of good cheer. She wasn't sure how she felt about flirting with a squishy invertebrate, but their banter shed some insight to his state of mind. He was starved for mental stimulation and chaffed at the restraints placed upon him in Syracuse. She could empathize to some extent—too many weeks spent exclusively with the elder council made her stir crazy as well. At least she had her sorcerous workshop and her minions, something that fed her need to create. If he was telling the truth, Halldix hadn't tinkered in months.

Cassie looked at herself in the mirror and practiced her facial expressions. She might have too many vertebrae and not enough arms, but that wasn't going to stop her—she had an octopoid to reel in. If she played her cards right, she could leave Oswego with a lot more than a few pebbles.

Chapter Four

The carriage rolled down the road, pulled by a team of galloping horses nearing ever closer to the royal estate of the Kingdom of a Thousand Islands. The Church of Parkour's flag whipped in the wind. The mother of the stride kept looking to the other seat out of habit, expecting to see Chandi reading a book, but alas, she was alone save one member of the Order of the Guard stationed inside the cab. This was Khiri's first visit since Dexter's death, and Chandi's absence was another reminder that times were changing.

As was his custom, Tallis greeted the carriage, but his demeanor was softer. In the loss of their shared lord, the steward's tacit truce had an air of leniency for one who had known Dexter, his estate, and his steward in another time. The abbess met his gesture with an almost casual bow, lacking the rigid formality that implicitly created space between two sentients.

She entered the kitchens to greet Claudette and to poke around the pots and pans for hints of dinner. The two women greeted each other as the old friends they were before getting on with their work. She inquired how Chandi was doing; Khiri informed her that Pathfinder Choudary was inducted and continuing with advanced training. Claudette shook her head and pressed a packet into the abbess's hands. "They may grow up too fast but they're never too old for shortbread." The tigress smiled and nodded, carefully placing the crumbly cookies in her pocket.

Khiri was summoned by Her Royal Highness Amelia Marie Winchester Montague, who was waiting in the blue room with tea. The tigress walked through the familiar corridors and came upon Emma, dressed for company but not ceremoniously. Decorum demanded the abbess give a formal bow and address her by her title, after which Emma bade her to take a seat and have some refreshments.

"Chandi isn't here with you?" Emma inquired after pouring.

"Regretfully no. She recently started her tracer training and felt it too soon to take time off for travel. However, she sends her condolences on the loss of your father and regards for your own speedy recovery." Khiri accepted a small plate of sandwiches and filled tarts.

Emma did her best to hide her disappointment—it had been a turbulent winter with the loss of her father, the birth of her son, and Stephen's travels to assess the kingdom. "Hardly any reason for regular visits now that there is no tribute to pay," Emma remarked off-hand, alluding to the recent alienation of Unseen Waters for their contribution to rebuffing the wastelanders from the kingdom.

"She did ask me to relay a message regarding the possibility of a visit later this summer on the way to visit her family deeper in the kingdom. She is looking forward to meeting Baby Emery, but felt both you and baby could use these early days to get to know each other without constant visitors." The abbess sipped her tea.

Emma's face lit up. "Oh, how thoughtful! Yes, I will send her a letter to arrange the details." The sleeping baby cooed in his bassinet, echoing his mother's delight. "Isn't he just an angel? He's a good eater and sleeps through most of the night."

Khiri regarded the small pink bundle with tenderness. "He has your father's chin."

"Let's just hope he doesn't inherit his stubbornness!" Emma joked before pausing as her father's passing freshly arose in her mind. Khiri placed her hand on Emma's back and waited until the moment passed.

Emma pulled herself together. *I'm a mother and a queen, for goodness sake.* "But I didn't call you all this way to have tea and gush at my adorable son. I asked you here for your advice." Khiri tilted her head in interest.

"Stephen has kept in touch with his contacts in the Ontario League. They are doing great things in Ottawa since the end of hostilities, and that's what we want for the Kingdom of a Thousand Islands. What's the use of fighting other civilized people when we are all under threat from barbarians and muties? Instead of fighting each other, why not reclaim the ruins and turn them into productive real estate again?" Emma shrugged and shook her head.

"Our longstanding friendship with the Church of Parkour gives us keen insight on how the church could be a part of this vision. In order to transform the ruins, we must understand what's in them, and there is no sentient that can traverse the ruins like a runner with the Church of Parkour."

Khiri bowed deferentially. "Your confidence in the church's abilities are flattering."

"It's not flattery if it's true," Emma stated emphatically. "But before we can embark on such lofty goals, we have to cease fighting amongst ourselves. Papa loved a good war, but Stephen and I want peace in our time. We want to drum up support for ending the legacy of ceaseless conflict while the kingdom is united after the victory over the wastelanders." Emma smoothed the lines of her skirt before proceeding. "Therefore, we would like to petition the Church of Parkour to assist in peace talks with the Lordship of Fingers, our mutual neighbor to the west."

*****

Pathfinder induction was a simple affair: your instructors and preceptors signed off on your training, the prioress filled out the paperwork, and the abbess gave you a benediction and new clothes, including the mask and hood that completely concealed the runner except for their eyes—only pathfinders and tracers were allowed to wear them. Four of the recent graduates opted out of tracer training immediately after induction; Mira and Natalie found placements in the same sept somewhere in West Tennessee, Joshi was headed to one of the Confederated State of Ohio, and Finn was stationed at either the People's Republic of Quebec or the Quebec People's Republic—one spoke English and the other spoke French, but Chandi could never remember which one was which, not that it mattered to Finn because he was fluent in both.

Chandi was still getting used to it. It felt weird to be addressed as "Pathfinder Choudary" instead of Chandi. She was still a sister of the stride, but now she had a titled position. She wasn't sure what to expect from tracer training, but if the first week was any indication, it was mostly reading and writing essays about various topics that were not running: leadership, church organization, theology, psychology, effective communication, group dynamics, political organization under the shattered moon, etc. Then was advanced stillness and rituals, which involved a lot of inner reflection and self-enhancement to "better actualize your stillness and meditation." There was a reason the old adage was if you wanted to run, be a pathfinder; if you want to wax poetic about the art of running, become a tracer.

The difference between pathfinders and tracers wasn't just

academic. While some tracers embraced traveling from sept to sept, those that wanted to limit their scope had a much better chance of becoming sept leaders, placing themselves in executive positions that were technically available to pathfinders with experience but in practice were filled with runners who had a higher level of ordination. Tracer training also prepared them for the isolation of a traveling tracer; up to now, all forms of meditation and training happened in group settings. If you did better in groups, you were better off running as a pathfinder or becoming a sept leader as soon as possible after finishing tracer training.

The saving grace for most tracers-in-training was the running. Tracers-in-training still ran every day, but meditations became even more self-directed; they traded in preceptors for advisors—someone to guide you on what you wanted to accomplish rather than tell you what to do. Depending on your advisor and personal path, tracers-in-training could travel to different areas to hone their skills; Dora had been gone for nearly a week on such a trip.

Chandi almost lost it when she found out that Ryland was her advisor, but they both remained punctilious until watchful eyes were directed elsewhere. He was surprising strict for someone so laid back and parsimonious with his efforts. She wouldn't go so far as to call him lazy, but she would wager there was a good reason he was uncannily good at finding the most efficient path.

Chandi had just cracked open her next assignment, *Contemplations of Stillness*, when Lucy hauled herself into bed.

"Everything hurts," Lucy moaned from the top bunk.

"You're almost done with orientation," Chandi tried to cheer her up.

"I know you think you're helping, but that just means I have two more days of this," Lucy mumbled.

"Right, this is me stopping helping," Chandi muttered.

"Aren't you seeing Mika tonight?"

"Nope, he's on assignment—going where he's needed," Chandi answered matter-of-factly while she reread the same page of her book for a third time.

"You guys are two peas in a pod," Lucy teased.

"Aren't you going to see Willem?" Chandi directed her roommate away from scrutinizing her and Mika, whatever they were.

"That would require me climbing down, which is not going to happen. I'm staying in bed for the rest of the night while I question my life choices and pray for sweet death to deliver me from my pain," Lucy testified. "Plus, he had a meeting after dinner with his old preceptor."

"Dora?" Chandi's interest peaked. "Do you think he's in trouble?"

Lucy was quiet for a moment. "I don't think so. They already gave him his mask and hood, so he should be in the clear. He's so straight-laced and when he does veer off the path, he's super careful about it. Oh, speaking of which, he wanted me to give you something, but you have to come up here and get it."

Chandi laughed and climbed up the side ladder, accepting the linen-wrapped metal cube that had plagued Willem for months. Chandi lay back on her bed and examined it in the light. The four-inch stainless steel box gleamed. Each facet had unique intricate geometric patterns; no side was the same. One side depicted the sun with the opposite side the moon; another facet featured interlocking rings juxtaposed by a square circumscribed circle on the other side. The final pair of sides featured a pyramid with an eye and a six-sided star. The container itself was a piece of art.

Chandi gently shook it and heard something rattle inside. Pretty little boxes holding unseen cargo? No wonder Willem pocketed it—it was just too mysterious to pass up. Chandi started twisting, turning, poking, and pushing; anything that elicited a change. Some things were always mutable, others were contingently so. For example, she could only rotate the moon if she pressed down on the eye and pyramid design. She quickly abandoned her reading for the puzzle box, and it wasn't long before Lucy had drifted off to sleep.

Chandi let her muscle memory take over once she found a multi-step combination until finally, she heard a click. The center of the six-sided star unlocked, revealing a hidden internal hinge. Chandi opened the panel and spotted something within.

She turned the box and dropped the black round faceted gem onto her palm. It didn't sparkle per se, but there was a subtle luster as she turned it in the light. Chandi was about to call for Lucy when her palm started to itch. *How curious?* was the last thought Chandi had before she passed out.

*****

A refreshing breeze blew through the warm evening air. Chandi opened her eyes; the cloudless sky sparkled with stars. It took a moment for her to realize something was wrong with the sky: the moon was whole. Its creamy bright surface was mottled with swirls, just like the pictures she had seen in Dexter's library. Staring at its majesty in person was breathtaking, like the difference between listening to a recording of music and feeling it course through your body during a concert.

"It's a harvest moon," an introspective voice spoke from behind. "The ancients use to revere it, calculate when it would come and center holy celebration around it. Who could blame them?"

Chandi sat up in the tall grasses that swayed in the gentle wind and caught sight of the speaker. He was tall, at least six feet if not more, with broad shoulders pulled back proudly. In the light of the full moon, his alabaster skin gleamed in the light and the peaks of his muscles cast shadows across his chest. Golden collars and necklaces lined his neck and his long ear lobes hung low, weighed down by intricate filigree earrings. His curly locks tumbled from beneath his headdress, and a diamond-shaped bindi sat perfectly in the middle of his forehead. The corners of his mouth were upturned and his eyes were mischievous—he was accustomed to being adored. In one hand, he carried a lotus, in the other a club.

"Moonstone," Chandi called him by name. "I always figured you were female.

"I chose a form you would understand," he replied.

Chandi scoffed, "My parents are devotees of the old ways, not me."

"Yet, you know who I am," he quibbled. "But if it would make you more comfortable..." He transformed before her eyes, losing more than a foot in height. His bare chest blossomed with breasts, covered by colorfully embroidered silk robes that draped to the ground and dangled from his arms. His curly locks straightened and took on a glossy sheen, and his eyes lost their folds and narrowed, becoming almond-shaped. "Is this better?" a soft feminine voice left her mouth.

Chandi grew suspicious—why present itself as a person now...a Hindu moon god and a Chinese goddess nonetheless? "What do you want?"

"I'm here to warn you. The apocalypse is coming."

Chandi loosed a curt laugh. "You're a little late. The moon has been shattered for ages."

"No, not the breaking of the moon. The rise of Atlantis is

at hand."

"Excuse me?" a bewildered Chandi uttered. *How can you apocalypse the post-apocalypse?*

"The waters will rise and claim the earth. All will perish and the cycle will turn again," she stated it like it was fact.

"Why are you telling me?"

"Because I can help you escape the cycle of reincarnation under the shattered moon. I can make sure that this time, you run fast enough."

Chandi noted her turn of phrase. "What's the catch?"

Her pained face hardened with spite. "I was shattered into pieces like the moon itself and changed against my will." Her expression softened. "If you make me whole again, I can open a rift into another time, one where the moon is whole, like this."

"And why would you do that for me?"

"Because you are the only one capable of making me whole."

"Even if I wanted to," Chandi carefully qualified, "how exactly am I supposed to do that?"

Moonstone turned and looked the pathfinder in the eyes. "You are changed, like me."

Chandi momentarily became lost in her beauty before the words soaked in. "What's that supposed to mean?"

Moonstone's face furrowed. She turned her rapidly from side to side. "You will see shortly. There isn't time to explain everything. I won't be able to manifest myself this clearly again.

Remember this: make me whole and I will help you escape. Now you have to wake up."

"No!" Chandi yelled. "You are going to tell me everything. No more messages through cryptic dreams."

"Chandi, you must wake up," she beseeched.

"I want answers!"

Moonstone grabbed her shoulders; Chandi could smell the jasmine off her hair and skin. "If you don't wake up now, you won't wake up. Wake up now!"

Chandi woke abruptly and found herself still in bed. She was still wearing her clothes from the night before, except they were drenched with sweat. The candle was still burning, but down to its last. Her copy of *Contemplations of Stillness* lay open on the bed, as well as the open cube. Chandi shook it to see if the gem was still inside, but the stainless steel box was silent. She checked the bed, patted down the sheets, and looked on the floor. Nothing.

Chandi searched her backpack for something roughly the same size and weight of the gem and found a hunk of metal caught on the bottom. She dropped it into the middle of the six-pointed star and closed the latch just as Lucy made noises above her. "How is it already morning?"

"Morning devotion waits for no one." Chandi did her best to keep her voice level. She quickly changed her clothes and splashed clean water on her face. She could still smell the sweet grass and jasmine on her hands.

Chapter Five

Brother Gerald prepared the room for the elder council, making sure each seat had a copy of today's agenda and a pencil. Left to their own devices, someone would inevitably forget to bring a writing utensil and interrupt the meeting to ask for one, prompting a search of the other council members. This was the advantage of having an experienced steward—he knew how to anticipate and avoid problems.

He placed cups and pitchers of water—there weren't many items on the agenda, but a quick and discreet glance told Gerald that the discussion was going to be vigorous nonetheless. Debating was thirsty work. He replaced the short candles with new ones and clipped those whose wicks were growing long before lighting them. He lit the incense and blew out the fire once the flame took. As the resin smoldered, the fragrant smoke unfurled.

The senior steward had just finished straightening the chairs when the first of the council members entered the chamber. The room gradually filled and he checked the time. As he spun the prayer wheel, the room became quiet. Brother Gerald took the small mallet and struck the chime, marking the beginning of the meeting.

Brother Gerald led the council through the gamut of procedural business with ease before turning the meeting over to Councilwoman Dunn for resolution of old business and introduction of new business. Cassie, who had laid her papers out with precision beforehand, rose to address the council. "Esteemed members of the council, I have news from Oswego. Our second contact with the Lordship of Fingers went without incident. Our primary objective has been achieved: we have recovered the remains of Moonstone and it has been neutralized. Unfortunately, it is not a renewable resource that can be mined, as we once hoped. Rest assured, we have recovered as many lunar spirits as possible, and they are back at the lab for analysis." There was a series of mumbles and nods around the table.

"As you are aware, our octopoid liaison is now king regent, and His Tentacled Majesty Halldix Kepoi has agreed to consider a more permanent church presence in the Lordship of Fingers. Therefore, I would like to petition for new business, namely, the establishment of a cloister house in Oswego." A hushed awe hung in the scented air.

"During our last expedition to assist with spirit activity in the area, I found a pre-existing structure that could be used with minimal modification, a sept leader suitable for the location, and a provisional agreement with Lord Kepoi that only needs council approval to be made official. I have also taken the liberty of drafting a preliminary start-up budget for such an endeavor." Cassie handed a stack of papers to Brother Gerald for dissemination.

It was a brief document, only three pages long with an appendix, downright bare bones by church standards. Still, all the standard clauses and legalese that protected their commitment and assets were there. Councilwoman Ratch's eyebrow raised. "What does this clause about 'all terrain around and near Oswego' refer to?"

"Ah, that is part of the new initiative I'm hoping to spearhead at Oswego Cloister House. As you recall, our initial search for Moonstone failed, and it was only after we widened our parameters to aquatic terrain that we found it. Therefore, I would like Oswego to become a training ground for amphibious running for sentients who are so blessed." More papers rattled as elders stopped their reading at Cassie's suggestion. "I have identified a tracer of amphibious background who also has experience running as a pathfinder; I think she would make an ideal sept leader for such a project."

"Running in water?" Councilman Pollack scoffed.

"Why not? Sorcerers run the otherworld," Councilman Luther countered.

Councilman Kolas lowered his glasses. "What does this octopus want in exchange?"

"Tribute from the ruins; as a tinker, he feels his subjects

have long ignored the potential hidden among the ancients' ashes." Cassie found it hard not to crow at what she considered her greatest coup de grace in brokering the deal.

"That's it?!" Councilman Kolas inquired in disbelief, adjusting his glasses to review the document in his hands.

"Section II, subsection 3, paragraph 2," Cassie directed their attention. After a moment of silent reading, even Councilman Kolas couldn't find fault with the document.

"Thank you for your report, Sister Cassandra," Councilwoman Dunn broke the stalemate. "Everything looks in order. I motion to vote on the proposal to establish the Oswego Cloister House in the Lordship of Fingers. Do I have a second?"

"Seconded." A hand raised on the other side of the table.

"Let the record show the motion is seconded by Councilman Nichols. All in favor for entering into this agreement with the Lordship of Fingers for the establishment of the Oswego Cloister House, please raise your hands." Cassie held her breath as the vote was called; she knew springing it on them as a rider to old business was a gamble, but she had to strike while the iron was hot.

"Let the record show the ayes have it, eight to five with council members Pollack, Kolas, Rogers, Cheng, and Webber in dissent. Motion passed," Councilwoman Dunn announced. "Congratulations, Sister Cassandra. You have a lot of work to do." Cassie slowly released her breath and gave a formal bow. "Now, on to the next item..."

*****

Halldix glided through the water, pulsating his limbs in rhythm through the nippy waters of Lake Ontario. It had been a week since the Church of Parkour's envoy left the area, but he lingered, enjoying the freedom of the frontier. He still received regular messages from his advisors; their tentacles' reach was great. Even still, the girdle of power seemed less constricting here. After His Tentacled Majesty took care of business, he could shed that mantle and simply be Halldix Kepoi, tinker. Halldix ordered his Rochester lab to be moved to Oswego a few days after arrival, and he was finally able to submerse himself into the inquires that piqued his interest before his uncle's death.

His advisors were in various states of disbelief when he informed them about the agreement made with the Church of Parkour. There was a furious epistolary exchange, in which Halldix would rebuff their objections and explain how allowing the church into Oswego was *not* only not harmful but beneficial to the Lordship of Fingers. As expected, the bulk of objections were merely shorthand for "it's unoctopoid," or "I wish you had consulted us first."

Halldix knew he should be more concerned with their dissatisfaction, but the prospect of tinkering with tech out of Oswego buoyed his spirit despite the whisper campaign that was surely taking place in Syracuse. Halldix was highly amused that the very traits that made him a darling at court when he was merely Lord Kepoi, son of Thenor, suddenly made him unoctopoid as its king regent. He hadn't changed, merely his title.

After a hearty meal, Halldix dove into his lab and examined the most recent batch of pearls of making. Using a bead as a mold for nacre deposits was a relatively new process he employed after hearing about how the ancients cultured pearls in salt water. It took a little experimentation to adapt it for fresh water, but it was worth the effort. Not only was the resulting shape more pleasing to the octopoids, but the production time was considerably faster. His first batch was a rousing success: lustrous gray spheres that produced a prodigious amount of water. The second batch, however, was not so inspiring, neither in appearance nor water production. They were cultured in the same incubator for the same amount of time, but these were smaller and duller. *Perhaps the temperature of the water is to blame, or maybe the seed material is lacking*, Halldix theorized.

Each of the tinker's arms moved independently, opening and closing drawers, picking up pieces, and writing notes as he mulled over his next course of action. Moving forward, he would continue taking measurements of future pearls produced, both in size and water production, as well as measuring the water's temperature twice a day all year round to see if there was any correlation between quality and environmental conditions.

Even though they were not as fine as the first, the second batch was still acceptable. Halldix checked his notes; the first load was seeded with rock found on the edge of the Oswego River. Ah, Halldix remembered finding that stone—an unassuming thing, except that it was painted bright pink. He had read of the ancients painting rocks as a form of art and thought nothing of it at the time. He dug into his kit to see if he had any more pieces from the specimen and found a small bead. "Let's see if there is anything special about you," he murmured as he rolled the rock in his sucker and began running experiments.

*****

As the abbess called Unseen Waters into morning devotion, Chandi fought a strong urge to scratch. Her skin seemed hypersensitive, begging to be rubbed at the persistent hint of a prickle. She hadn't squirmed this much at morning devotion since she was a tenderfoot.

She left Lucy to pathfinder orientation and quickly sprinted toward the ruins—she didn't want Willem to find her and ask her about the cube. Tracer trainees weren't supposed to run solo at Unseen Waters, but she wasn't up for company today. She had no idea what she was going to tell him. "There was a giant black gem inside, but I lost it" wasn't going to go over well. She would launch a more exhaustive search when Lucy wasn't there; at least it would rattle when shook, in case either he or

Lucy picked up the box.

Chandi picked up the pace and let her meditation through movement flow; she started to feel like herself. She pulled up her legs as she leapt on top of a piece of plascrete, planting her feet and springing into the air. She grabbed onto a wall and cat pulled herself up. Dora's exercises had built her upper body strength considerably and now she used her legs because it was more efficient, not because she needed to. She dropped and rolled over her left shoulder, finding her feet with ease.

She was still unpacking her conversation with Moonstone. First, she felt it was a little unfair that no matter form it took, it was stunningly beautiful. *How distracting is that?* Second, the whole point of showing up in a form that talks was to communicate more clearly—telling cryptic apocrypha and saying "you'll see" or "you'll figure it out" wasn't helpful. In Chandi's book, that dream still counted as totally donked up. Third, what the hell did it mean by "changed"?

Chandi executed a wall spin, directing her deeper into the ruins. There was a dry brittleness to Watertown, as if the morning dew hadn't touched it. The further she ventured, the more devoid of life it became—even the birds stopped chirping their morning song. She felt a knot form in her stomach as she came upon a cluster of walls. *This is why they tell you not to run alone!* she chastised herself. She stepped off the walls in a triple reverse tic-tac, altering her course toward Unseen Waters.

As she made contact with the ground again, she felt a ripple course through her. It wasn't strong enough to knock her down, but enough to make her pause and take note. She blended into the darkest shadow and took stock of the ruins. Her green eyes darted back and forth from the slit in her mask—all was still. As she came out from her hiding place, a glimmer in her periphery caught her attention. *That wasn't there before.* Chandi cautiously approached until she spotted the source of the light—a small carved wooden frog that glowed a soft light purple. The pathfinder came to an abrupt halt and gingerly touched it. It didn't hurt, but the itch in her fingers became more intense. She pulled off her hood and used it to pick up the frog and place it in her backpack before rearranging the hood over her head. She made another sensory sweep of her surroundings before taking the most direct path back to the Monastery of Unseen Waters.

*****

After accepting the position at Unseen Waters, Ryland was upgraded from a room in visitors' quarters—which was little more than a bed and table—to a suite: part workshop, part living space. Ryland surveyed his room—comparable to Jackson's but smaller than Bartholomew's—and it seemed gigantic to the tinker-runner who had grown accustomed to carrying everything he owned on him or in him. It took him all of five minutes to unpack.

He was just about to toast his new accommodations when a frantic knock edged his door open. "Ryland, are you here? I went to your room in the visitors' section and they said you had been moved." He recognized the voice of his newly assigned tracer-in-training.

"Ah, Chandi! What do you think of the new place?" Ryland turned and saw the ashen look on her face. His carefree tone became serious. "What's wrong?"

Chandi closed the door behind her and slung her backpack off. "I need you to look at something and tell me if I'm going crazy." She dug around and held out the carved wooden frog in her left palm. "Is this glowing purple?"

Ryland left his drink on the table and approached her. He punched her in the arm and Chandi recoiled. "What the hell, Ryland? That hurt!" She felt tears well up in her eyes.

"I'm sorry, Chandi. I had to be certain," he rapidly apologized and raised his hands in surrender before gently wiping the tears from her cheek. Chandi gasped at the sight— her tears on his finger were a muddled gray. "Sit down. I need you to tell me everything."

Chapter Six

Lucy trudged down the hall, dreaming of her bed. Sure, she would have to climb down for dinner, but she was so sore, it seemed worth it. She kept telling herself it was just one more day of orientation and then she'd have a normal routine. She panicked when she heard the ruckus coming from her room but calmed down when she heard Chandi's muffled voice within. "Hey, what have I told you about putting a sock on the door if you are going to have an afternoon delight?" she teased as she opened the door.

Chandi's entire bed was tossed with pillows and sheets pulled in all directions. Chandi straightened up abruptly. "Lucy! You're back early."

"Sister Abatha took pity on me in the gardens and let me go early," Lucy spoke coyly, nodding at the figure crouched behind Chandi. "Do I need to leave you two alone?"

Ryland cleared his throat and stood. "That won't be necessary. I was helping Chandi look for something and I think we've exhausted the search. Don't you, Chandi?" Chandi bobbed her head in agreement. "Why don't you rest up and we'll start training bright and early tomorrow."

"Sounds like a plan," Chandi chirped and plastered a smile on her face.

He crossed the room to the other side of Lucy before giving Chandi a kind, reassuring look. "Remember what I told you. It's going to be okay."

As soon the door closed, Lucy was on her in a heartbeat. "Holy crap, you're *doing* your advisor? This is amazing! I want to hear everything." Lucy plopped down on Chandi's rumpled bed. "I never would have pegged him as your type, but to each their own."

"Lucy, I'm not sleeping with Ryland," Chandi emphatically set the record straight. "I was freaking out because I thought I lost something important, and he was here to help me look for it."

"With his tinker vision?" Lucy inquired with a sufficient level of woo-woo in her voice.

Chandi laughed. "Something like that."

Lucy looked deflated at the diminishing prospect of good gossip in her near future. "Well, did he find it?"

"No, but he doesn't think it's a problem."

"You know, my version would have been more interesting." Lucy bobbed her head side to side as she changed topics. "Have you seen Willem today? I've been meaning to ask him about his meeting with Dora, but we keep missing each other."

"No, I haven't seen him all day."

"Drat. Did you make any progress with his cube last night?"

"Nothing helpful," Chandi answered honestly.

*****

Ryland rolled the stainless steel cube around in his hands. Chandi had shown him how to open it, and he repeated the sequence in the privacy of his room. The center of the six-sided star gave way, and out rolled the hunk of metal Chandi had stuffed in there this morning. He closed the now empty box and set it aside for a drink.

He and Bibi were supposed to christen his new room, but he was far too distracted to have company tonight. The sight of Chandi's gray tears tore open old wounds. He thought back to his own conversion; he preferred that term over "infestation." He was in a coma for ten days with the worst dreams he had ever had. When he woke, he no longer felt right in his own skin, and in an instant, his entire world turned upside down. Running was the only time he was almost normal, and when the church told him he could no longer run, he ran from the church.

But things were different now. The church had created a space for tinker-runners. Chandi didn't have to make the choices he had. And she had him as an advisor; that was more than he'd had. Ryland thought taking this position was going to be a step back—advise a couple kids, keep things working at the monastery, and spend the rest of his time playing in his new workshop and picking Watertown at his leisure. He allowed himself a second of self-pity before snapping out of it. He was a tracer of the true path—he went where he was needed, and this pathfinder was going to need his advice and training.

He opened the folder procured from the records room and dove into Chandini Choudary's background. She cleared toxins, including radiation, saw well in low-light conditions, and—scrawled in Jackson's hand—dampened spirit activity. No real disciplinary record to speak of, which was pretty amazing considering how long she'd been here. She was one hell of a runner—ten out of ten flags on her pathfinder trials. He skimmed the notes from her instructors over the years with her preceptor's glowing appraisal toward the end. Coupled with what he knew about her from their visit to Oswego three months ago, it added up to an extraordinary picture. And now she was a tinker.

Of course, his first tracer trainee had to be a wunderkind. The fact that she was only out overnight was a miracle. Ryland started rubbing the stubble alongside his chin—he knew he was out of his depth. He was going to have to call in reinforcements, but first, he and Chandi had to get her story straight. Then he would go to the abbess and inform her about Chandi. Once her tinker abilities were out in the open, he could go to Bartholomew about the rise of Atlantis—whatever the hell that was—and then to Jackson about Moonstone. He didn't have to do this alone, but he had to do it in the right way, in the right order, for Chandi's sake.

*****

Chandi planted herself on the ground and looked up at the moon. It was torn almost in half with one side mostly intact and the other broken into different-sized chunks. Even if you could knit all the pieces back together, there weren't enough parts to make it whole again, not like the moon Chandi saw in her dream. Chandi wasn't even sure it was a dream, but that sounded less scary than a nanite-induced fugue state. She tried not to think about it too much—Ryland told her that stressing would make the itching worse.

She knew she would have to eventually tell Willem his cube got confiscated. Luckily, Ryland seemed unconcerned about busting Willem and more interested in where the cube came from. She was actually feeling better about the whole thing now that she had more facts—if Willem or Lucy had touched the black gem, they could have died. Chandi wasn't sure if Moonstone's warning to wake up actually saved her, but she wasn't ruling it out. If what Moonstone said was true, it could have been keeping her alive for its own selfish motivations, which begged the question—would it keep its end of the bargain once it was made whole?

Chandi heard a familiar shuffle in the grass behind her.

"Where have you been hiding out? Lucy's looking for you."

Willem stooped down next to her. "How did you know it was me?"

"We've been training together for the better part of a year—you have a very distinctive footfall pattern."

"You are so weird," Willem lay back and joined her in stargazing.

"You don't know the half of it," Chandi muttered. The quiet between them settled as she waited for Willem talk.

"I may be leaving," he finally broke.

"What do you mean?" she calmly asked for clarification. After the past twenty-fours she'd had, this didn't even hit her top five things to freak out about.

"Dora offered me a job as a pathfinder. She's secured a position as a sept leader for a new cloister house, and she thinks I would be a good fit."

Chandi was confused. "I thought she was still in tracer training?"

"Not after her last training trip. Apparently it was some sort of extended interview, so she's taking the oath and leaving in a week's time."

"And where is this new cloister house?" Chandi fished for more information

"Not far west of here, in a place called Oswego, just on the shoreline of Lake Ontario."

Chandi impressed herself when she managed to keep her

face still at the mention of Oswego. "You said you might be leaving. Does that mean you haven't decided?" she probed.

"It's a great opportunity, Chandi," Willem gushed. "There are ruins that haven't been picked through. Can you imagine the kind of finds I could cash in at pathfinder rates? What am I doing here—reading books and writing papers? Dora's cool— she'd be my sept leader—and it's really close to Unseen Waters. It's only a day by carriage; I could take all my time off to visit here."

"But..." Chandi anticipated the qualifier.

"The location is going to be used as an amphibious training ground. There isn't any way that Lucy would be assigned there after she finished pathfinder training, even if she wanted to skip tracer training."

"I'm assuming you haven't told Lucy yet," Chandi deduced, "so why are you telling me?"

"Because I needed to talk to someone. I've been churning the same points in my brain all day and I can't make heads or tails of it. It seems perfect, but if there isn't even the possibility of Lucy being there, what's the point?"

Chandi nudged Willem in the ribs. "I think you are burning through all your good talking points on the wrong person."

Willem sighed. "Think of this as a rehearsal. At least you aren't punching me or crying."

"I could punch you if it would help..."

"Anyone ever tell you you're all heart?"

Chandi let out an honest laugh from deep in her belly. After the day she'd had, she needed it. "Go find Lucy and tell her what's going on. If she's important enough to you that you are having these kinds of thoughts, she's important enough to be included in the decision-making process. And be sure to keep the 'it's pointless without you' part."

They lay in companionable silence until Willem mustered his nerve. Chandi thanked her luck that he was so distracted about his news that he forgot to ask about his cube.

Chapter Seven

The mother of the stride alternated between sitting back in her chair and leaning forward as Ryland went through the particulars of his tale. As agreed, he did all the talking, and Chandi stood there, nodding in agreement when necessary. When he finished, the abbess steepled her fingers and tapped them together. "So let me get this straight. Pathfinder Choudary found this cube in the ruins but wanted to unearth what was inside before turning it in. When she opened it, a black gem fell out but it wasn't actually a gem, but instead a conglomeration of nanites that invaded her body." She paused to drum her fingers a few more times. "Then she fell into an overnight coma and awakened as a tinker."

"That's the long and short of it," Ryland confirmed.

"And the gem is gone. It's literally inside of her," Khiri reiterated.

"That is my belief," Ryland stated.

"And you're certain she's a tinker."

"The initial assessment was consistent with that finding."

"Out of curiosity, what kind of assessment is that?" the

abbess seemed genuinely curious, but Ryland still felt it was a trap.

"She sees purple and cries gray tears full of nanites, which is a common presentation in new tinkers who haven't learned to control their nanites. I know that sounds less than scientific, but that's a definitive result in the tinker realm," he made his case plainly. Chandi gave Ryland a sideway glance and was relieved to see he was actually nervous. At least she wasn't the only one.

"I've never heard of an overnight coma," Khiri commented.

"It is unusual, Abbess. My speculation is that it has something to do with her innate ability to clear toxins. If tinker conversion creates a toxin in the host's body as a byproduct, then the ability to clear toxins would reduce recovery time. But that is just a theory," he qualified.

Khiri gave a non-committal bob of the head before motioning to the stainless steel cube Ryland had placed on her desk. "And this cube isn't dangerous anymore? No one else is going to get infested and fall into a coma?"

"Preliminary analysis suggests there is no further technological risk," he replied.

"And what preliminary analysis was that?" she inquired.

"I had Jackson get close to it and see if it gave him the willies," Ryland answered. "It's low-tech, but reliable."

Khiri rubbed her temples and took a deep breath in and out before addressing the pathfinder. "Chandi, do you want to continue with tracer training?"

Chandi noted her lack of formality despite Ryland's best efforts to keep this official. "Yes, Abbess."

"Then it's settled. You will continue your training with Brother Ryland as your advisor and I will notify the appropriate channels."

"With the mother of the stride's permission, I would like to conduct some more extensive investigations with local resources before bothering the main house with the matter," Ryland interjected. "Any report made at this junction would be inherently incomplete, which seems unnecessary considering the pool of talent within Unseen Waters that could shed more light on the situation if given enough time."

Khiri sized up her newest instructor. Ryland's hindbrain flared up as the tigress's pupils focused on him. "Ryland, you may coordinate with our local scholars and sorcerer before filing an official report." He noticed two things: her address was personal and now *he* was doing the paperwork. "But if there are any changes or unforeseen complications, you will notify me at once. Both of you. Is that clear?"

"Yes, Abbess," the tinkers replied in unison.

She dismissed them from her office and they left in a hurry, taking the win where they could. Neither Ryland nor Chandi thought it was best to mention Moonstone or the rise of Atlantis until they knew more. After all, if the world were really coming to an end, surely the church would have caught wind of it with their network of runners. There was no need to stir the abbess if it came to nothing after their research.

Chandi was just glad it was out in the open. Although she was capable of keeping a secret, she preferred not to. It felt too much like lying by omission. She followed her advisor to their next port of call: Brother Bartholomew's. Ryland had reached out to the scholar before breakfast but did not tell him of the particulars. The curious old bird cleared his schedule and found a visiting scholar to take his Tenets of Faith class.

After the expected sentiments of concern, the scholar was fascinated by the twists and turns. He was pleased that Chandi kept her guard up with Moonstone—it was always gratifying when sentients took your advice, especially the young. It was edifying to know they were really listening, not just hearing. There were too many threads to follow just one, but the scholar always loved a good challenge. He would have to spend some time with his source material to unearth information about alternate timelines, Atlantis, and otherworldly-touched items that underwent technological transformation, but there was one mystery he could help Chandi solve immediately.

He opened two tomes and pulled out a myriad of bookmarks, rapidly flipping back and forth before approaching Chandi. "If it's not too trying, I want you to think back on the black gem you touched. Was it complete black? Or was it a dark green or a mottled color, possibly a dark gray?

"Jet black," she answered.

Bartholomew pulled out a few markers and continued, "Was it smooth like a polished rock or hard with facets like a gem?"

"Definitely a gem," she replied with surety. Ryland smiled at how much joy the scholar was getting from the process of elimination.

"Did you hold it in the light?"

"Yes, briefly before I passed out."

"When you held it in the light, did it sparkle like crystal or cut glass?"

Chandi wavered. "It shimmered in the light, but it wasn't like when a light passes through a prism or reflects off a window…nothing that bright. It was more subdued."

Bartholomew had narrowed it down to two. "When the light shined on it, did it radiate in a six-rayed star, like this?" He traced a pattern in her palm with a feathered finger. Chandi shook her head from side-to-side. Bartholomew closed one book and turned the open tome around so Chandi could see. "Did it look like that?"

"Yes! That's it," she pointed to the rose cut.

The scholar triumphantly announced, "My dear, you have been touched by a carbonado, more commonly called a black diamond."

*****

Chandi's brain felt like it was going to pop. When Ryland said he needed to assess her basic knowledge of science and technology, he failed to mention how wide his definition of "basic" encompassed. It was like taking every science exam ever at once. He promised an easier day tomorrow, but that did little to help with her brain-dead state tonight.

Their section of the long communal tables was conspicuous quiet. Chandi did little more than grunt, and she was too mentally exhausted to figure out the right way to tell her friends that she was infested with nanites. She was pretty sure that didn't make for polite dinner conversation. Lucy and Willem kept giving each other looks across the table with a nervous tension, leaving Hanu and Sura to do most of the talking which quickly turned into Hanu's one-man show of stories and antics while Sura surreptitiously held his hand under the table.

Chandi was surprised when Lucy came back to their room later that evening. She figured Lucy and Willem had a lot of talking to do, but perhaps everything that could be said had already been uttered. Lucy plopped herself on Chandi's bed, and Chandi held her arms open to receive her friend. Her dark brown eyes were red and puffy, but she didn't have any tears left to shed, at least for now. Lucy shifted to blow her nose and settled next to her roommate.

"So Willem told you?" Chandi spoke softly.

"Last night," she mumbled. "It's not fair. Things were going so well and now it's all a mess. I can't tell him not to take the job— it's a great opportunity that was made for him—but I don't want him to go and he doesn't want to leave me, so it's a no-win situation. He can't both stay and go."

Chandi had the beginning of a notion. "Why not?"

"What do you mean 'why not'?" Lucy stared at her like she'd sprouted a second head.

"I mean, why can't Willem do both? Why can't he continue his tracer training remotely in Oswego? He'd have to get Dora to sign off on being his adviser instead of his sept leader, which wasn't an option when she was still in tracer training but is totally doable if she's a full tracer."

Lucy sat up, intrigued.

"Willem would still get to take advantage of this position in Oswego without the assignment being permanent. If something should change a year from now..." Chandi alluded to Lucy completing pathfinder training, "he could leave Oswego and come back here to train. Or, you two could try to find a sept with two open positions."

"You can do that?" Lucy perked up.

"Mira and Natalie did. Granted, they had to go to West Tennessee, which is a total snoozeville, but they managed it."

"And if it ended up that the job wasn't what he thought it was, he could always come back!" Lucy grasped Chandi's gist.

"And he would probably get more days off if he were still in school—no production quotas when you are still in tracer training," Chandi added. "Granted, he would still have to leave

Unseen Waters, but he'd have his foot in the academic door with an easy path to return, if that's what he wanted to do."

"You are amazing," Lucy stated simply.

Chandi chuckled darkly. "I'm a wreck."

With her sadness lessened, Lucy could see Chandi's distress more clearly. "Are you okay?"

Chandi blurted, "Well, in the past forty-eight hours, I've been infested with nanites, seen some weird shit in the ruins including but not limited to a glowing purple frog, been punched really hard by my advisor, cried gray goo, and quizzed three times to next Sunday. Oh, and I've committed to visiting my parents who I haven't seen in twelve years and a sister I've never met, so I am about as far from okay as you can get." Fat gray tears formed in the corner of her eyes. Chandi wiped them away and held them up on her fingertips. "See? How messed up is that?"

Lucy didn't recoil. Instead, she put her arm around Chandi's shoulder. "Is that why your advisor was here yesterday?"

"Yeah, he was making sure there wasn't anything dangerous left in here."

"In here? You got infected by nanites in here?!" Lucy exclaimed.

Chandi smirked. "Willem's cube."

"You got it to open?"

"Yeah. Yay me?" Chandi cheered sarcastically.

"Oh, I could kill Willem for nicking that off the battlefield," she cursed vociferously.

Chandi laughed, this time with more levity. "A second ago, you were mooning over how much you wanted him to stay."

Lucy shook her head as she cradled Chandi. "The more you love them, the more they drive you insane."

*****

The whispers and subtle color shifts under the skin flared through Syracuse as the members of the six noble families heard the news—the Lordship of Fingers granting land to vertebrates? It shook all strata of society. The bold applauded His Tentacled Majesty, extolling the move as raising the stature of the kingdom by connecting them to the larger world under the shattered moon. They argued that it was only the ruins on the edge of their kingdom, leftover land taken from the Kingdom of a Thousand Islands and already inhabited by vertebrates. It was a small concession of little importance in their mind.

There were those that were simply in shock. Their myopic view of the world started and ended in noble waters and they could not fathom Halldix's retreat to Oswego. Why would anyone leave Syracuse? It had everything an octopoid needed.

The moralists argued that the kingdom was losing its cultural identity. They clamored on about dilution of the octopoid way, about the slippery slope of interaction with vertebrates. First it was trade, then it was communication, now it's comingling and surrendering territory. What was next—cutting wide doorways to accommodate them when a three-inch hole was all a real octopoid needed?

Lastly, there were the pot-stirrers, those that enjoyed watching the spectacle: the old-fashioned fuming, the provincial swooning, the progressives pressing forward. They rallied for Halldix and scorned him with equal measure depending on their audience, simply for the pleasure of watching blue blood pump more vigorously.

But in the hidden corners of Syracuse, there were octopoids making plans. No longer satisfied with words and chromatophores; they felt action was needed. Their thoughts bordered on blasphemy, but wasn't a king who was unoctopoid a heresy in its own right?

Chapter Eight

"The first thing you need to understand is that working technology is a valuable commodity, which makes being a tinker valuable. We are the only ones that can fix tech and create new things from it," Ryland started his lesson. "It also makes the world under the shattered moon more dangerous. Generally speaking, tinkers regularly deal with substances that have a greater consequence of failure. So the first thing we are going to do is make sure you don't kill yourself." Chandi found his bluntness both terrifying and oddly reassuring.

"There are different levels of expertise depending on how much you want to invest in tinker training, with not running and exclusively tinkering at one end of the spectrum, and knowing just enough about tech to spot the good stuff on a run on the other end. Where you want to be is your call to make. Don't worry about the church…no matter what you decide, they will find a way to send you where you are needed.

"I've heard back from Brother Bartholomew about your concerns with your recently negotiated agreement of service with the church," Ryland paused to consult his notes. "He feels that the language is worded in such a way that should you want to pursue tinkering for tribute, you could serve in that way with all the permissible clauses of refusal stipulated in effect. He made a note of the relevant passage if you want to review it." Ryland handed her a sheet of paper with the phrase "innate abilities in service to the church, any of its members, allies, benefactors, or installations," written in the scholar's hand—you don't get more innate than being infested with tiny machine life.

"That said, you have a good grounding in how science used to work. If you want to extend your tinker training, I think you have a solid foundation to start on simple repairs that require mundane science and work your way up to the more complicated stuff."

Ryland exhaled heavily. "Now this lavender frog you found, that's a whole other game. That is the realm of super science. It plays by a completely different set of rules. I will teach you the different shades and grades for spotting tech, but if you really take to tinkering, it's vital for building new creations or executing repairs when you are lacking the mundane parts. In my opinion, it's the creative heart of tinkering."

Ryland thought he had covered his opening remarks but paused to make sure he hadn't missed something before opening it up. "Okay, do you have any questions?"

"So when will I be able to manifest things out of my hands and repair plasma guns on the spot?" Chandi asked with lurid fascination.

Ryland smiled. "That's going to take some time. After we go over the ground rules—"

"So I don't kill myself," she interjected.

"—then we have to work on controlling your nanites. When you have better control over them, we can start working on repairs and move into the purple stuff. This isn't like any of your other innate abilities, Chandi. You don't get all the benefits by them simply being on in the background. The only thing you get for free is seeing purple and crying gray. Everything else is a skill you have to hone, like the way you've treated running."

"How long did you apprentice?" she probed the boundaries that had shut her out earlier. She knew Ryland left the church to train as a tinker and eventually returned, but that was all.

Ryland crossed his arms and eyed her, contemplating what to do about her relentless curiosity. "I know what you are doing, Chandi. And only because the past couple of days have been hell and I feel bad for punching you so hard, I'll give you five questions. But then my past is closed and I'm the only one who gets to open it. Deal?"

"Deal," Chandi perked up. "How long did you apprentice as a tinker?"

"Five years," he responded.

"You were gone from the church for five years?! Wait, don't answer that. That doesn't count against my five." Ryland did his best to hide his amusement as she conjured her next question;

he remembered when five years seemed like forever. "Which do you like better: running or tinkering?"

"They fulfill two very different needs. I would wager that being a runner makes me a better tinker and vice versa, but I can't imagine choosing one over the other. It isn't a competition, and anyone that tries to tell you it is wants something from you," he cautioned.

Lines formed around her eyes as she squinted in thought. "Are you sorry you rejoined the church?"

Ryland was quiet for a while, giving the question serious thought. He was thankful he'd limited her to five. Finally, he answered, "No."

Chandi nodded—the answer rang true, but it took Ryland a long time to come to it. "Okay, I'm good."

"But that's only three questions," Ryland pointed out.

"I've saving the other two for later," she spoke with the confidence of youth. "So, where do we start?"

Chandi took careful notes as Ryland reviewed caustic materials, basic chemistry and what you should never mix, how to neutralize strong acids and bases, and what is flammable and explosive. He glossed over radiation and poisons due to her inherent capacity to clear toxins, but cautioned her to be aware of them should she find herself running with a sept that was not so blessed. He reviewed electricity, conductivity, and magnetism, "Sentients underestimate the power of magnets, but trust me, you don't want to put your hand between two super magnets when they want to come together," Ryland warned her.

He showed her diagrams of circuitry and how to safely navigate electricity. "*Never* work on live wires," he stressed, and she wrote it down and underlined it twice. Chandi frantically tried to copy all the pictures but Ryland stilled her hand. "You'll see this again. This is just to make sure you know what it looks like and when not to touch it."

"So I don't kill myself," Chandi grimly replied.

"Exactly."

Chandi's anxiety marginally increased and she fought the urge to scratch her leg. "Will the itching stop?"

"It will get better as you learn to control them. Like I said, it tends to get worse when you are stressed, either physically, mentally, or emotionally. It comes when you are manifesting objects or absorbing them, and sometimes when you are working with super science, depending on how high a grade the material is. But honestly, you just sort of get used to it."

"I'm sure you're right, but I just can't imagine getting used to this. I feel like I'm sharing my skin with something other than me." Chandi dropped her notebook and surrendered, rubbing her nails in long strokes over her lower leg.

"Follow me. I think we have covered enough about how not to kill yourself for one morning. Let's move on to the next lesson." Ryland motioned for her to leave her things; all she would need was herself. She followed him out to the courtyard and into the now empty main hall. He positioned two mats beside the prayer wheel facing each other.

"Remember when I said that being a runner made me a better tinker?" Ryland began. Chandi nodded. "That's because as a runner, I know what stillness is, how to find it, how to grow it, how to focus it, and how to be still in it. I know it feels impossible to find stillness again with your new friends, but you can with practice and the right frame of mind." Chandi looked at him dubiously but indicated that she was listening.

"You aren't alone anymore. It's like a colony, and you are their queen," Ryland tried a metaphor.

"Like bees?" she asked quizzically.

Ryland shrugged. "Sure, like bees. You may not have chosen to share a body with them, but you can determine what kind of ruler you are going to be. The natural inclination is to fight them, and I've seen tinkers try to force their nanites into submission, but that's just exhausting. They are a part of you now. Why would you choose to spend the energy to constantly fight yourself?"

Chandi nodded politely but her furrowed brow told Ryland this wasn't working. He tried to bring her back in with a religious parallel. "Being a tracer of the true path, I opted for the most efficient route, the one that had the least resistance. In a matter of speaking, I flowed like water over my nanites." Chandi seemed to intuit that better than the bees.

"When I chose to stop fighting my nanites and work with

them in a symbiotic relationship, things got easier. I took care of them and they took care of me. I made our existence mutually beneficial. When that happened, I learned how to control them because they let me. Does that make sense?"

Chandi mulled over his words. "It's like Applied Tenets of Faith—you can redirect the energy that's directed against you."

"Yes!" Ryland got excited that he was gaining ground. "That's all the itching is. It's energy, and once you learn what stillness feels like with your nanites, you will be able to direct that energy, dissipate that energy, and when necessary harness that energy." Chandi's brow unfurled in comprehension.

"First, we start in stillness. When you feel an itch, release that energy and find the stillness," Ryland and Chandi assumed the meditative position on the mats. Ryland spun the prayer wheel and watched Chandi close her eyes before dropping his lids.

*****

The bleary-eye faces of the elder council lit up as Councilwoman Dunn called the last bulletin on their agenda. "Last piece of new business. We have a petition from Khiri Tham, mother of the stride at the Monastery of Unseen Waters. She has been approached by Her Royal Highness Amelia Marie Winchester Montague of the Kingdom of a Thousand Islands to initiate the peace process with the Lordship of Fingers.

Additionally, Her Royal Highness has expressed interest in future collaborations with the Church of Parkour to 'make the ruins productive real estate again.'"

The weariness that hung in the air was suddenly lifted as council members sat up in the seats, setting aside their respective distractions. "I'm sorry, who is Her Royal Highness Amelia Mary…" Councilman Nichols voice dropped off as he failed to recall her full name.

"Her Royal Highness Amelia Marie Winchester Montague is the sole surviving daughter of His Royal Highness King Dexter Albert Winchester VI," Brother Gerald dutifully read from the ledgers he had marked for the meeting. "She, along with her husband Stephen Montague, ascended the throne of the Kingdom of a Thousand Islands after Dexter died battling the Laughter at the End of Time."

"By the founders, they're still around?!" Councilman Kolas marveled.

"As long as there are ruins, there will be the Laughter at the End of Time," Councilwoman Ratch grimly spoke.

"Dexter finally died in the saddle, did he?" Councilman Pollack snidely remarked.

"No," Cassie piped up. "Heart attack." A reverent hush fell over the room where the youngest councilmember was well into their fifties.

"Wait, if Dexter had a daughter, why were we holding out for his distant cousin to become of age?" Councilwoman

Rogers inquired.

"The council deemed her unviable at the time," the senior steward filled the gaps in their memory. "Apparently, she's two years married and has just given birth to her first child, Emery Albert Montague." The council mumbled in agreement; Cassie fought the urge to roll her eyes.

"Who are they currently at war with again? Dexter's girl, I mean." Councilman Nichols still hadn't bothered to learn her name.

"Kingdom of a Thousand Islands: currently at war with the Lordship of Fingers and the Hudson-Mohawk Demarchy. Last year, they sued for peace with the Ontario League," Brother Gerald read from his book of accounts.

Councilwoman Dunn opened the floor for thoughts; Councilwoman Ratch raised her hand. "How close are we to opening the cloister house, Sister Cassandra?"

Cassie sat up. "Less than a month. Our sept leader has already recruited some pathfinders and Unseen Waters has generously lent us construction equipment now that their wall repairs are complete. I am in the process of petitioning their resident tinker to finish converting the building."

Councilwoman Ratch lowered her glasses and her shrewd eyes shrank with the removal of the lenses. "I propose we establish the Oswego Cloister House first and springboard into peace talks after His Tentacled Majesty gets his first taste of tech out of the ruins. Sister Cassandra, you'll be active in the area, do you think you can spearhead both initiatives?"

Cassie bowed deferentially. "Certainly, Councilwoman Ratch. I will go where I am needed."

Councilwoman Dunn waited for other ideas before closing the floor and calling for a vote. It passed 10-3, motion carried.

*****

Jackson methodically checked his gear before donning his dagger, belt buckle, and components. He wasn't sure what he was going to find, but that niggling feeling flared up when Chandi recounted her tale for Bartholomew and him. It took every ounce of willpower to stay seated in the room with Chandi's unbridled nanites—it made him appreciate how much Ryland must rein them in when they were together. He was tasked with investigating any possible connection between Moonstone and Chandi's pearl of making. Normally, he wouldn't put much stock in the dreams of a seventeen-year-old, but Chandi wasn't you average sentient. She was touched by Moonstone, and he felt duty-bound to investigate. He sent Cassie a message, asking if their plan had come to fruition. With any luck, she'd found Moonstone in the waters of Oswego and his work would be done.

But that wasn't the part of Chandi's story that stuck in his craw. There was something in her description of the ruins that rubbed him the wrong way. The desiccation she described rang true to what he'd noted recently, and the palpable ripple that passed through her ate away at some deep part of his brain, hinting at a memory of a memory. That's what got him thinking and onto this fool's errand.

Aren wasn't pleased with Jackson's request. None of the Order of the Guard that survived the wasteland attack would go near the pit, but Jackson insisted. He had a hunch he had to check out, but he had no idea where their remains were left. After reminding the captain of the guard of his commitment to protecting everyone at the monastery from the otherworld, Aren agreed to ask for volunteers, but the stubborn goat stipulated that if no one came forward, he was not going to order anyone to approach that foul place.

Jackson walked through the courtyard and past the front gates where a lone soldier bearing the Church of Parkour's symbol on her arm stood. They greeted each other with terse nods, and she led him into Watertown. It was an area they didn't patrol, as the abbess had placed a quarantine on it after they dumped the last of the slain wastelanders. If the tales were to be believed, the pile of corpses filled the small gorge.

The first thing that bothered Jackson was the lack of animals nearby. It was one of the main reasons the abbess prohibited pathfinders and tracers from training here—the presumed increase in predators and scavengers that would be drawn to the meat. The next thing he noted was the lack of smell. According to his guide, they weren't far, and the stench of a hundred rotting bodies should have been overpowering given that the spring thaw was at least one month past. But nothing prepared either the sorcerer or the soldier for what they saw when they approached the pit. To their horror, the gorge was completely empty.

*****

"What do you mean, they're missing?" the abbess quizzed Jackson.

"I mean, the pit is empty. No bodies. No bones. No nothing," he spelled it out clearly.

Her eyes narrowed. "Are you sure you were at the right location? If memory serves, you were sleeping off a concussion while they were carting the bodies off our doorstep."

"I had a soldier from the Order of the Guard that was there that night escort me. She swore up and down that was where they put the bodies."

The abbess sat down at her desk, pulled out two tumblers, and filled them with a generous amount of amber liquid—she had a feeling they were both going to need it. Jackson polished off his portion in one go.

"What does the otherworld have to say about it?" the abbess sipped hers slowly.

"That's the really creepy thing—not only were there no signs of animal life, the otherworld was silent, too." Jackson didn't have the words to describe how unnerving it was for a sorcerer to hear nothing from across the veil. "Do you have any ideas of what this could be?"

"It could be nothing. Ruins change and maybe that serendipitously took care of our waste disposal problem," the abbess speculated, but it was a little too neat for her tastes. Plus, she didn't like that whatever was happening spooked her sorcerer. "Let me reach out to the scholars of the main house. If this is a herald of something coming, they will know."

Chapter Nine

Willem had traveled to Oswego with Dora two weeks ago, and the rest of the sept she recruited trickled in as the days passed. The first to arrive were the twins: Flo and Telly. They had similar coloring and finished each other's sentences but were otherwise as different as night and day. Flo was gregarious and the first to pass the flask, while Telly was bookish and kept to himself. Hailed from newt linage, there were the only ones of true amphibious stock besides Willem and Dora—Sister Cassandra's vision was not based on biologic classification but practical terms. The Oswego Cloister House was where runners who could seamlessly traverse both land and water were to run and eventually train others so blessed.

Clara was the next to arrive, a pathfinder with fish heritage who had gills along the side of her delicate neck. Then came Hendrix, an honest-to-god merman whose legs became a tail when submerged in the water. He was incredible in the water, and his familiarity with three-dimensional movement made him equally good at navigating the ruins on dry land. The last to arrive was Nelli, a sentient with a little sea turtle in her; while technically of reptilian heritage, she was at home in the water. Dora had all the pathfinders spend more time in the water to acclimate themselves. This was a new chapter in church exploration, and they were the pioneers.

Willem emerged from the water, breathless and exhilarated. He hadn't realized how much he missed it after all the years he'd spent exclusively on land. He wasn't the fastest or the most graceful of swimmers, but his ability to breathe underwater meant he would have plenty of time to improve. Willem dried himself off and made the short trek back to the cloister house, a twentieth century brick and mortar elementary school the church had refurbished to suit its needs. Complete with a kitchen, dining hall, laundry, and black top for training, there were plenty of empty classrooms that could still be converted into dorms or meeting rooms, and the grounds were surrounded by a wall. He stopped by the kitchen for food and one of the kitchen staff snuck him a small between-meal snack.

Unlike Unseen Waters, the cloister house used lay people for the mundane tasks, leaving Willem more time for running and training. He missed Lucy and the monastery, but he could get used to the lightening of chores. The tradeoff was more responsibility over religious maintenance: all the necessary rituals to sustain and protect the cloister house fell on their sept. Morning devotion waited for no one, especially out here.

The physical repairs to the structure and wall went quickly once the heavy equipment and construction crew came from

Unseen Waters, and Cassie took care of establishing the spirit wards. All they were waiting for was a visit from the tinker, due any day now. Cassie had requested Ryland, because he was good and he was close. She had high hopes that he could get the old solar panel on the roof working and find some way to harness or store that energy for essential functions. She generally went out of her way to avoid technology, but the time she spent in Oswego led to more evenings with Halldix, and he had an endless fascination for the stuff. It was his keen eye that spotted the solar panels on his visit to the cloister house.

His Tentacled Majesty didn't say as much, but Cassie got the impression he was pleased by the sept's connection to the water and intrigued by the difference in the nearby vertebrate population when the cloister house opened. Between the cooking, cleaning, mundane maintenance and upkeep, and food production, the cloister house offered employment to families that lived hand-to-mouth. While the initial supplies for the larders and dry goods were carted in by the church, eventually that money would be entering the local economy. Now they had someone to sell things to, sentients that shared a similar material culture with them unlike the octopoids. Halldix was finally starting to see what the vertebrates needed to thrive and was slowly coming to the realization that it was not that dissimilar from octopoids, albeit wrapped in different skin.

*****

They assembled in Ryland's quarters—even though Bartholomew's was technically bigger—because it was unencumbered by years of possessions, research materials, and equipment. "You really need to invest in some personal touches," Jackson prodded Ryland. "It's pretty utilitarian in here."

"Maybe a plant?" Bartholomew kindly suggested.

"Forgive me for the lack of decor—I've been a little busy making sure my tracer-in-training is all right." Ryland distributed drinks to his guests.

"How is Chandi doing? She doesn't stop by as often as she used to now that she no longer goes on tribute trips and training provides her a prodigious amount of reading," the scholar inquired as he sniffed the amber liquid and took a sip.

"She's going to be okay," Ryland predicted. "Once she made the connection between tinkering and running, she's been plowing through training."

Bartholomew chuckled fondly. "You should have seen her as a child. You couldn't stop her from running, jumping, and climbing over everything."

"I've started her on simple repairs to hone her fine motor skills. She seems to like the methodical precision of it," Ryland couldn't hide the pride in his voice. "But that is not why we are here. The abbess wants this report before I leave for Oswego. So tell me what we've got."

Jackson and Ryland yielded to their elder brother of the stride. "Let's start with Atlantis," the scholar began, gathering his papers. "I was able to get more information from a colleague that did research in the Thalassocracy of New Greece. While it provided a wealth of information in general, I'm uncertain how helpful it will be to Chandi. Atlantis is a fictitious island written about by the oldest of the ancients, a person named Plato. In his writings, the Greeks rebuffed an attack by Atlanteans and used it as allegorical evidence that Greek society was superior."

"Wait, so they made up stories about imaginary places they defeated in battle to prove how great they were? I'll be the first to admit that I'm a little rusty on my ancient Greek history, but weren't they fighting all the time amongst themselves?" Jackson puzzled.

"I don't know. Seems pretty consistent with the new Greeks I've come across," Ryland quipped. "Why would you expect their progenitors to be any better?" His comment elicited a smirk from Jackson.

Bartholomew cleared his throat and continued. "In the story, Atlantis fell out of favor with the gods and goddesses, who submerged the entire island into the Atlantic Ocean. It would have remained an obscure footnote, were it not for a later revival where other artists and writers appropriated Atlantis and added their own meaning to it. Basically, Atlantis became shorthand for any advanced civilization that is lost to history with utopian overtones."

"So where does the rise of Atlantis come from?" Ryland chimed in.

"Well, modern ancients had a lot of cultural references to Atlantis, and some of them dealt with the return of Atlanteans, either because explorers went into the deep and found them, the island itself rose from the waters, or Atlanteans surfaced from the deep. However, I couldn't find anything about rising waters that bring about the rise or return of Atlantis." The bushy eyebrows on his strigiform face was clearly displeased. "Most of the other information I received from my colleague was about the ancients speculating Atlantis was inspired by an actual island that sank into the sea and where that might be."

"What about the ability to travel to another time?" Ryland moved onto the next item on his list.

"That I had an easier time researching." The scholar shuffled his stack of papers. "It is generally accepted that multiple timelines exist, but the evidence of them is always retrospective. We can only know what is in our timeline, and we only receive information about other timelines from castaways of another time or from conflicting historical accounts left by the ancients. We are always looking backward, trying to piece together when timelines diverged, but we cannot look laterally or into the future. Additionally, there is no support for the notion that traveling between timelines is something a sentient can purposefully do; castaways had no agency in their arrival to our timeline. There were some theories about trying to travel into the past before the apocalypse, but scholars came up against the same problem: which past?"

"So, it's possible to travel to alternate timelines, as evidenced by castaways, but we don't have any working examples of sentients leaving our timeline for another?" Ryland grappled with the scholar's account.

Bartholomew pulled out his pipe and nodded. "Exactly, but Jackson may be a better person to ask. Moonstone is a conduit to the otherworld; I'm not sure what it is capable of in that capacity." He lit the dried leaves in the bowl, signaling his presentation was over.

Jackson placed his half-empty glass on the table. "Anything's possible, but that isn't consistent with what we know about Moonstone; it is a conduit from the lunar otherworld to Earth."

Ryland jotted a few things down and checked off another item from his agenda. "Thank you, Brother Bartholomew, for your insights. Jackson, what have you got?"

Jackson sat back and started talking, "I got word back from Cassie. The remains of Moonstone were found in the shoreline waters of Lake Ontario a few miles west of Oswego. Four small pebbles, to be exact. Her lab confirmed they are spiritually inert, and Moonstone is considered neutralized as far as the elder council is concerned.

"In light of her most recent vision, I thought it would be best to look at Chandi's pearl of making. I reviewed all the testing results from Bartholomew. I'll be honest, it didn't make a lot of sense to me, but the important thing is that I don't think it's active in an otherworldly sense, either. I'll know better after you and Chandi go to Oswego—when she'll gone from the monastery for a longer period of time than running Watertown." Jackson shuddered at the thought of spending more time with the nanite-infused gem.

"If it is Moonstone in there, it is entirely possible that the tech coating the bead is acting like a containment chamber, blocking its ability to interact with the otherworld. If that is the case, I would advise against any more attempts to remove the nacre." Jackson looked pointedly at Bartholomew.

"If her pearl of making is a sorcerous center in a tech shell, what would that make it?" Ryland picked Jackson's brain.

"If that were the case, it would make it technosorcerous, as it has both components. That sort of item would be highly concerning if it were crafted by a wizard who could synergistically use both sorcery and super science to create some seriously powerful and dangerous items, but that doesn't seem to be the case here. Additionally, if there is no way to confirm that theory without removing the tech that is hypothetically containing the otherworldly activity, I think it's best to let sleeping dogs lie," Jackson concluded.

Ryland reviewed his notes. "So, the rise of Atlantis is a dead end, traveling out of our timeline to an alternate timeline is theoretically possible but no one knows how to do it, and if

Moonstone is inside of the pearl of making, we should leave well enough alone. Is that the gist of it?" The brothers of the stride were in agreement.

"Okay, I'll write up my report and inform Chandi of our findings and that she'll get her pearl of making back after we return from Oswego. Thank you for your help in this matter. To the founders." They raised their glasses and toasted to the conclusion of a productive meeting.

*****

Chandi intently listened to Ryland's account, breathing a sigh of relief as he reviewed the finer points. "So it was probably just a crazy dream while I was in a mini-coma?" she ventured a hypothesis.

"Probably. I remember having some very vivid dreams during my conversion and with your recent history with Moonstone, it would make sense that your subconscious wove it into your dreams," Ryland speculated.

"And even if Moonstone is at the core of my pearl of making, it's okay. It's not going to hurt anyone in there," she double-checked.

"That's what Jackson thinks, but he'll know more when we get back from our trip." Ryland turned his attention to her workspace in his quarters. "How's it going?"

Chandi's face twisted. "Well, I got this part of work, but I can't figure out what I did wrong over here." She pointed with the tip of the delicate screwdriver.

Ryland moved the light and took a closer look, wiping the grin off his face before coming back up. "You have the gear flipped the wrong way."

"Seriously?!" Chandi yelled.

"Don't sweat it. We all have to start somewhere, and you really are doing quite well," he reassured her.

"Thanks," Chandi replied, and started undoing her work. "At least I'm not crying gray anymore. Well, mostly."

"Are you doing your meditations?" he queried.

"Yes," she retorted petulantly.

"Three times a day?"

"At least twice," she answered truthfully, "but if you count morning devotion, then yes."

He started on his report while Chandi finished her work. Both of them muttered under their breath while they worked, blissfully ignoring each other's chatter as they focused on their respective tasks. Chandi slammed down her tools on the table and raised her arms in the air victoriously. "It's fixed!" She twisted the knob and the gears moved lockstep. "Unless you need me for something, I'm going for a run before dinner." She handed Ryland his tools.

"You keep it. You're going to need to start your own toolkit. Bring it with you when we go to Oswego, and I'll show you how to absorb it on the ride there so you won't lose it."

Chandi nodded and pocketed the small screwdriver before leaving her advisor to his paperwork, longing for the stillness found in movement.

*****

"Ry, come back to bed," Bibi beckoned when she awoke in the middle of the night and saw him hunched over his desk with a lit candle.

"I just have some paperwork to finish before I leave tomorrow. You go back to sleep," he called back softly.

"Don't you think I woulda done that already if I coulda?" she asked rhetorically. She smoothed her coat and made a cape from his light blanket as she rose from his bed. "Is this the report for the abbess? I thought you finished it before we went to bed."

"I just want to go over it again. I don't get a do-over if something's wrong, and the last thing I want to do is irrevocably screw up Chandi's life over a clerical error."

Bibi put her hand on his shoulder. "How many times have you been over the report?"

"A couple," he replied vaguely.

"It's sweet that you care so much, but leave well enough alone and get some rest. Morning devotion waits for no one, and you've got a long carriage ride tomorrow."

Ryland put an arm around her waist and rested his hand on

her hip. "Is that Texican for 'stop being a damn fool'?"

She laughed. "Somethin' like that."

Ryland put everything back in its place and blew out the light. "You know, Jackson says this place could use some personal touches. Maybe a plant?" He curled against her soft fur.

"Ry, you know you gotta work to keep a plant alive," Bibi teased him.

"Well, maybe a cactus."

Chapter Ten

Chandi was more excited about this trip than she cared to admit. She couldn't remember the last time she'd stayed at Unseen Waters for four months without traveling. Once the monastery had been alienated from the Kingdom of a Thousand Islands, Chandi was no longer obligated to conduct monthly tribute visits, giving her time to focus on her training while Brother Bartholomew helped her obtain continued support for her family and village through tribute service on her terms. She was so concerned with not being taken advantage of that she hadn't realized how much she liked to travel until it was gone.

Lucy grilled her roommate one last time before sending her to the carriage. She wanted the inside scoop on the situation in Oswego—who was there, were they prettier than her, how was Willem, and if he looked adequately homesick. Chandi reassured her for the third time that she had packed Lucy's letter for Willem and joked that the "no sex in my bed" rule still applied, even if it wasn't Willem. "Give him a big hug for me," Lucy instructed as she relinquished Chandi.

"Will do, boss." Chandi faux-saluted.

Once they were on the road, Ryland started quizzing her on the different shades of purple, forming various objects in his hand and having Chandi name the hue. She had gotten most of them right, but the slight difference between close tints of purple could be tricky. What was the material difference between lilac and lavender? Eggplant and plum? A little more or less blue or red and you've got a completely different kind of programming within.

"What do you do if you're a tinker that's color blind?" she interjected her non-sequitur after correctly identifying a mauve pair of scissors.

Ryland absorbed the scissors back into his hand and grunted. "Not sure. Maybe they see a different color instead of purple? As long as they could tell the difference between shades, I guess the same rules apply, only it would be really hard to apprentice with a tinker when you can't see the same colors."

"Wouldn't the words still be the same?" Chandi mused. "They would just go their whole life thinking glowing magenta looked an awful lot like mundane chartreuse."

Ryland paused. "You're a weird one, Sherlock."

"So I've been told," Chandi affirmed and pulled out her new screwdriver. "I believe you were going to show me how to absorb this."

Ryland collected his thoughts. "As you know, things that glow purple are special. They are infused with nanite programming, and that's what makes them glow to tinkers. It's their way of advertising what they are, by glowing different hues with the intensity indicating different grades. When you absorb a glowing object, your nanites effectively save the program for you for later use. When you materialize that object, you are reproducing the item with its programming. With me so far?"

"Save coming in, reproduce going out. Got it."

"If it's glowing and you can touch it, you can absorb it, regardless of size and weight, because all you are doing is saving a program. As a general rule, the bigger the item, the more difficult it is to absorb it, but there is not an implicit correlation between size and power."

"Start small, and nice things can come in small packages. Check."

"This is one situation where controlling and training your nanites comes into play, because they are doing all the work. Essentially, you touch the object and imagine it absorbing into your hand. The nanites will do the rest."

"That's it?" Chandi sounded dubious.

"Well, it sounds simple, but it's harder than you think. It can take a little time and coaxing at first, but as you get better at it, it goes faster and smoother."

Chandi held the screwdriver flat in her open palm and closed her eyes. She could feel her nanites buzz with excitement. Chandi found her stillness and directed their energy to her hand, visualizing the screwdriver sinking into her. She felt a surge in her palm, and the tool was no long there when she opened her eyes. "Did it work?"

"Well, it isn't on the floor," Ryland ribbed her.

Chandi emitted a very high-pitched sound in glee. "Okay, so how do I get it back out?"

"Well, you do the opposite. You imagine the object in your hand, and it will appear."

Chandi closed her eyes again and took a few deep breaths to still her pounding heart. She found her stillness and imagined the tool in her hand and soon felt its weight on her palm. "That is so cool."

"Eventually, you will be able to do it with little effort and you won't even have to close your eyes, but that comes with practice," Ryland coached.

"And I can do this over and over as many times as I want?"

"Yes, but if you ever use that piece to conduct super science, it's gone. You won't be able to materialize that particular object again because you altered its programming," Ryland qualified his answer.

"But if it's just programming, why can't my nanites just keep a copy of the original?" Chandi griped.

Ryland shrugged. "I didn't make the rules, I just follow them."

"What if you forget what you've absorbed?" Chandi inquired.

"What do you do when you are having a hard time finding

something in your backpack?" Ryland posited.

Chandi wobbled her head. "I shake everything out."

"You can do the same with your absorbed tech. As you get more familiar with your nanites, they may be able to help you organize things so you don't have to dump out your entire inventory to find what you are looking for."

Chandi seemed pleased with her progress and spent the rest of the ride to Oswego playing with her newfound ability.

It was nearing night when the carriage pulled up to the walled compound flying the Church of Parkour flag. The original decorative wrought iron metal gates—superimposed on banded wood to offer more defense—opened at their approach. "Brother and sister of the stride, welcome to the Oswego Cloister House," Cassie greeted Ryland and Chandi as they descended from the carriage. "I trust you had good pathing." The Order of the Guard unloaded the sparse baggage—two tinker-runners travel light—before tending to the horses. "We have rooms ready for you and dinner will be served shortly." Chandi waited for her advisor's nod of approval before taking off to find Willem.

Ryland examined his surroundings. "Cassie, look at all this. This is all you, isn't it?"

"Isn't it exciting? I finally feel like I'm building something of my own instead of taking care of everyone else's stuff. I'll give you the full tour in the morning and point out some of the things that I was hoping you could fix."

Ryland's nose twitched. "Since when do you know anything about tech?"

"Well, Halldix and I have dinner every now and then when I'm in town, and I've picked up a few things," she replied nonchalantly. "When he stopped by the cloister house to meet Dora and take a look at the place, he may have pointed a few things out and explained how they could be useful if they were working."

Ryland narrowed his eyes and intensified his gaze. "Cassie, are you seeing His Tentacled Majesty?"

"Don't be silly, Ry!" she exclaimed. "You know just as well as I do they die after mating. I'm just working an ally for future benefit, that's all." She hooked her arm into his. "Now come inside and get settled before dinner. We have a lot of catching up to do…like how you're a teacher now." Ryland let himself be led and chose not to comment on her conspicuous lack of discomfort at his nanites.

*****

"Chandi, what are you doing here? Not that it's not nice to see a friendly face," Dora remarked.

"I'm here on behalf of the church in a tributary capacity, and Brother Ryland happens to be my advisor, so it seemed wise to share a carriage," Chandi replied simply; she let her eyes tell the rest of the story.

Dora laughed. "Well, your presence is a boon. We can use all the help we can muster to get this place up and running. Another mind at morning devotion is always welcomed," she warmly greeted her before gathering a bowl from the communal pot. Although Dora had always been kind, Chandi was not accustomed to this level of familiarity. It was startling, but not unpleasant. Up until recently, Dora was her preceptor, and now she was just another sister of the stride. She hadn't really thought of Dora as a normal sentient up until now. "Has Willem introduced you to everyone?"

"In his own way," Chandi ribbed her friend.

"I gave her the rundown," Willem defended himself. "The twins, the merman, the hare, and Clara."

"The hare?" Dora puzzled.

"It's the nickname my last sept gave me because even though I'm part turtle, I could out run all of them—you know, from the ancient's fable," Nelli explained.

"I hope you understand that I have to use your official name on reports, but otherwise, 'the hare' it is," Dora took a seat among her pathfinders, relieved to see them getting along so well. They were swapping stories from their past runs, one-upping each other's best finds, and comparing scrapes from the ruins. Although they had been assembled from different parts of the world under the shattered moon, they were all pathfinders and their stories shared a commonality that transcended geography.

Even though spring was well underway, the evenings could still be chilly and a fire was lit for comfort and cheer. After dinner, Dora retired to her quarters to finish some work and give her sept a chance to let their proverbial hair down without the presence of their sept leader. Telly found a cozy spot with adequate lighting before opening the book he'd stashed in one of his pockets. His sister pulled out the booze and a deck of cards, drawing the others into games of chance and skill while Willem and Chandi found a quiet corner to talk.

"They seem nice," Chandi observed from the side.

"Yeah, they're pretty cool." Willem shuffled his feet. "So, how's Lucy?"

"Officially? She doing great. She's really liking her pathfinder training and she's warming up to the others in her cohort," Chandi reported.

"And unofficially?" Willem asked nervously.

Chandi broke with Lucy's protocol. "She really misses you, but she's doing her best to put on a cheerful face and push through."

Willem released a deep breath that he hadn't realized he was holding until it was out. "Thank god! I miss her so much. It's not so bad when I keep busy, but during the quiet moments, everything reminds me of her. I found myself thinking that the dark red berries growing on a bush were the same color as her hair."

Chandi stifled a snort. "That's pretty bad. This is from

Lucy," she mumbled as she put her arms around him and squeezed. "And this." She handed him a folded paper. Willem stuffed it into his pocket—he'd save it for later when he had moment to himself.

"Do you like it here?" she gathered information under the guise of making conversation.

Willem didn't answer right away. "It's a little strange being the youngest one here...I was used to being the oldest at the monastery. All these pathfinders were with other septs, and I'm just out of training, so I feel like I have some catching up to do. But I'm learning a lot, and every day we run the ruins, I find something new and interesting. I like getting back in the water, too. I didn't realize how much I'd ignored it for land at Unseen Waters until I came here—ironic, considering the monastery's name. But I miss Lucy and you guys. Hell, I even miss Hanu giving me shit." His aside elicited a giggle from Chandi. "Don't you dare tell him I said that." She crossed her heart.

From across the room, Flo and Clara groaned as Hendrix slammed his cards down and declared gin. "You know, I never got a chance to properly thank you for figuring out how to make this work," Willem spoke softly. Chandi shrugged like it was nothing. "And I'm really sorry that I brought the cube into Unseen Waters," he apologized. "If I had known..."

Chandi gave him a befuddled look. "Willem, I don't blame you."

"You should. I would," he mumbled.

"It happened, and I'm going to be okay. Would you rather someone else had touched it and died? You? Lucy? At least I had some protection," Chandi reasoned. "But maybe this is a sign to stop pocketing shiny things directly from the ruins—better that they go through safety checks first," she dryly remarked.

Willem smiled. "I missed your sense of humor."

"You should try talking to Telly. I bet he's a hoot," Chandi suggested sardonically.

"You kid, but he's actually really cool. He just doesn't like big groups," Willem corrected her.

"Seven's a big group?"

"For him. And he's super smart—he's helping me get through my tracer reading. Can you believe he's read most of that stuff for fun?" Willem balked.

"Come on, you wanna show these geezers how gin is played?" Chandi nudged him lightly.

Willem laughed. "Sure, but if they offer to play for money, that's a warning to get out of the water—sure sign of sharks."

*****

"He's been gone for almost two months," Vissix started the informal meeting in the private pool. The forceful jets massaged the tension knots in her visceral hump. The four octopoids that shared her water flashed agreement under their skin.

"He does reply to our missives every day, and things are

being decided," Yakim came to his liege's defense.

"The Lordship of Fingers need a king regent who is present, who displays his power so that his subjects feel secure," Marbec commented.

Cabon scoffed. "What good is projecting power internally when you only have power inside Syracuse? Halldix is doing something bigger. He's pushing for octopoid visibility and recognition amongst other players under the shattered moon. Isolationism was fine when we were still swimming around the Finger Lakes, but we are in the bigger waters here. Lake Ontario is nothing to blow ink at."

"And how exactly is he doing that? Playing with his inventions? Pretending that he's a vertebrate?" Marbec shot back.

"You seemed pleased enough with the water jets he got working," Carbon sarcastically replied. "The Church of Parkour is employing nearby sentients to run their cloister house, boosting the depressed local economy. And Halldix has met the sept leader—she comes from the water," she argued fiercely.

"She may have had gills, but she still has a spine." Marbec flashed challenging colors along his visceral hump.

Yakim raised a tentacle. "Regardless how we feel about his initiatives, we would all like to see our Tentacled Majesty return to Syracuse. We can all agree on that, can't we?" A conciliatory wave of color blinked around the pool. "Well, that's not going to happen by fighting amongst each other. I think we can also agree that telling him to return hasn't yielded the desired result."

"What kind of king doesn't heed the council of his advisors?" Vissix sighed wistfully.

"A strong-willed king," Liam answered quietly. "Returning to Syracuse must be his idea."

"Good. This is good. We are getting somewhere," Yakim encouraged his cadre. "So what kind of thing would it take to entice him back?"

Cabon readjusted her hump. "By all accounts, he's quite content in Oswego. I'm not sure we can lure him back."

"Then what about a threat or problem that cannot be ignored?" Vissix suggested

A moment of silence before Liam spoke. "The brood. Tell him they're sick, and he will return. He is duty-bound to see one of Droxithal's fry to the throne, and for all of Halldix's faults, he loved his uncle."

"Won't he be angry when he finds out we have deceived him?" Vissix nervously asked.

"Maybe they could be a little sick…" Marbec mumbled quietly.

"You're talking treason," Cabon glowered.

"No one is talking treason," Yakim reassured her. "We are just taking a soak in the whirlpool."

Chapter Eleven

Morning devotion was a small affair compared to what Chandi was used to. As sept leader, Dora led them through the litany of stillness; it was more an invitation than a command. It lacked the strict obedience implicit in the abbess's presence—the tigress was a daunting figure, even in stillness. With just ten sentients, the ritual seemed more intimate as they radiated their collative will to the corners of the cloister house.

Chandi fell into the sept's routine, running with them in the morning after breakfast. While she was no stranger to parts of Oswego, she was content following Dora's lead and moving with the pack, intermittently stopping to investigate potential finds. Dora charted various routes while they had the benefit of Chandi's abilities, fanning out to cover as much of Oswego as possible. Chandi quickly grasped Willem's meaning—there was so much of the ancient's stuff lying around, she felt like a kid in a candy store, choosing which sweets to take home when her backpack was only so big.

As she was a visiting pathfinder on tribute, Chandi had the ability to keep what she found but relinquished most of it back to the sept. Pretty soon, they were going to have start tribute payments to the Lordship of Fingers. She marveled at the finds she decided to keep: a pretty charm for her little sister, and a bejeweled brooch of an Egyptian lotus for her mother that only needed a good cleaning. Before she left for Oswego, she'd replied to Emma's letter and made arrangements to stop over on the way to her parent's village on the Grass River. As the ancients would say, the die was cast, and she didn't want to show up empty-handed.

The sept returned and completed the ritual of repulsion designed to ward off beasts and other hungry creatures that wandered the ruins. After lunch as the sept swam in Lake Ontario during the relative warmth of the afternoon, Chandi snuck away to do her private meditations. She had come to think of it as communing with her nanites; it was her time to connect with them so they could work as a unified being. She returned to the lake to find everyone in good spirits. To her surprise, they were swimming nude. In retrospect, it made sense—clothing would only weigh them down and drag in the water—but that didn't spare her the initial shock of seeing Willem naked, which was only weird because she wasn't expecting it and they had been friends for so long. It did give her some insight into what Lucy appreciated about him physically, but Chandi could have lived without that tidbit of information. Willem, however, seemed unperturbed and beckoned her to join them. She shed her clothing and folded them neatly on a dry log before entering the bracing water. Before this, Chandi thought she knew how to swim, but after seeing the sept in Lake Ontario, she could only claim that she knew how not to drown. They each had their own method of navigating the water, but there was fluid grace in their movements that was breathtaking to watch. Chandi was especially intrigued at their physiologic adaptions. Clara's gill flaps opened and closed with each respiration, Hendrix's long legs had fused into a scaled tail that undulated through the depths, the twins had thin membranes that covered their vulnerable eyeballs, and Nelli's oar-shaped hands scooped through the water with ease when she closed her fingers.

Chandi had to keep coming up for air and called it quits when her fingers started to prune. She came out of the lake and grabbed a towel from the stack, drying off her skin and the moisture from her hair with vigorous rubbing before getting dressed and sunning on the bank. The water had been brisk but the sun beamed in the cloudless sky. Chandi fanned out her hair to dry in its unbridled warmth and closed her eyes from its unrelenting rays. She was only halfway through her first day, but so far, this was already the best tribute trip she had been assigned. It was a nice mix of doing necessary tasks and things she enjoyed, without the tedium. As the sun beat down on her, she entertained the notion of checking out Telly's stash of books after dinner.

*****

Ryland stroked his chin—Cassie had a lot on her list, more than he could possibly do in his three days there. Each time he tried to get her to prioritize, he found himself in a recursive loop.

"Ok, you say X is essential. What about Y? Can that wait until next time?"

"No, we definitely need that now."

"Fine. How about Z, can that be pushed to the bottom of the list?"

"Oh no, Z is pretty important. Better push that to the top."

After a couple of passes, Ryland realized this was an exercise in futility and approached it differently. He spent the better part of the first morning assessing the condition of each job, estimating the time it would take to fix it with regard to missing parts that needed to be scavenged first. He let her mull over his findings during lunch, essentially letting her pick the balance between what was easiest to repair and what was most beneficial to the cloister house.

Within those parameters, Cassie had an easier time assigning priority and Ryland spent the rest of the day fixing the simple things he could with just his knowhow, basic tools, and things the sept had already scavenged from Oswego. Ryland got to scratch a few things off his list and the cloister house had some running tech. He worked up diagnostics on the more challenging projects, compiling a list of parts necessary to make them operational.

As he was finishing up, a knock aroused his attention. Ryland reflexively held his hands together in front of his chest and pumped out twice before bowing at the sight of His Tentacled Majesty. Halldix mirrored him, impressed that a vertebrate knew the traditional gesture of greeting among octopoids.

"Please rise. There is no need for such formality when we are not in the presence of the etiquette squad," Halldix jested. "When I heard there was a fellow tinker on the premises, I had to come and meet you." The king regent held out a tentacle. "I'm Halldix Kepoi, son of Thenor, king regent of the Lordship of Fingers, but you can just call me Halldix."

Ryland took stock of him before gripping his extended limb, shaking it. "Ryland Simons, tracer of the true path of the Church of Parkour. While we were not properly introduced at the time, our paths have crossed before. Last fall in Oswego, I accompanied the healer sent by the church," Ryland bent the truth just a tad. "Although I take no offense at not being remembered, given the circumstances."

Halldix bobbed his visceral head in acknowledgement before looking past Ryland. "Am I interrupting your work?"

"No, I was just finishing for the day—taking stock of the work that needs to be done tomorrow."

"Mind if I take a look?" Halldix requested. "It will save

me from having to decipher what actually got repaired from Cassie's account later." His facial features morphed into what counted as a grin in the octopoid world.

So she's Cassie to him? Ryland took note as he glanced over his worktable—nothing valuable or incriminating. "Be my guest. It's pretty mundane stuff. I'm just knocking out the easy things."

Halldix locked three pairs of arms behind his back as he walked up and down the length of the table, curiously eying the machines and mechanisms. He was thrilled to be in the company of another tinker, someone who shared an implicit understanding of tech. Unlike Ryland or Chandi, who became tinkers later in life, Halldix was born that way, seeing colors that other octopoids could not. The early years were difficult because he was different from the rest of his brood and there was no one to teach him the rules. His kind was not known for embracing differences.

He was the rare self-taught tinker, and his nanites became his tutor and guardian, leading him to understand that he could repair and create things others could not while steering him away from dangerous combinations that would harm their host. To be able to speak to another tinker—much less a vertebrate one—and engage in a larger community of like-minded sentients was more than he thought possible as a young fry swimming the Finger Lakes.

Halldix spied Cassie's curly scrawl on a sheet of paper at the end of the table. "I fear apologies are in order—I am to blame for her enthusiasm regarding technology."

"No worries, Halldix," Ryland reassured him. "Cassie's always had robust desires…you simply gave her names for them." Halldix chortled at the observation. It occurred to the tinker-runner that he was going to get along just fine with this octopoid, and he accepted Halldix's invitation to show him his lab.

They spent the evening discussing the nuances of item repair and construction, the woes of their nanites, and approaches to fixing the solar panel at the cloister house, by far the most daunting of Cassie's requests considering how much was damaged and needed replacing. Ryland's was a learned vocabulary while Halldix's was more personal and intuitive, exposing the difference in their training. It was like having a conversation between a native speaker and someone who learned the language in school—intelligible to each other but there were things that got lost in translation and needed more time and words to understand their true meanings. At some point Ryland, pulled out a flask of whiskey and Halldix some spirits derived from seaweed, and the jocularity began in earnest.

*****

Liam circled the courtyard twice to make sure it was empty

before sliding through the narrow entrance into the hot house. It should be empty this time of night, but his failed attempt at a meeting last night diminished his daring. He had left the signal to meet after he left the whirlpool, but his contact must have failed to spot it. Liam returned tonight, hoping for a rendezvous. His persistence was rewarded when Lord Akkar's ropy body oozed in through the hole.

"Were you followed?" Liam asked the noble nervously. Lord Akkar answered with an indignant display under his skin. Liam remembered his station and flashed obsequious tones.

"Did the other advisors take the bait?" Lord Akkar grumbled.

"Hook, line, and sinker," Liam replied derisively, implying his fellow councilors were no better than fish.

The noble's visceral head blinked with delight. "And did Marbec disappoint?"

Liam bubbled a scornful chuckle. "He never fails to be a blowhard. I would attribute it to age, but he has always been cantankerous, even as a fry."

"Do you think him willing?"

Liam thought for a moment. "Yes. He truly believes the flotsam he spouts and therefore has no doubts about the righteousness of his actions."

"Then it is settled. We will wait for it to be done."

Lord Akkar was the first to leave and Liam waited an appropriate time before exiting himself. He calmed the rising well of excitement brewing inside him. History would determine whether they were heroes or traitors, but no one would say they did nothing.

Chapter Twelve

Ryland and Dora came to a compromise—she could have Chandi in the morning, but he would get her in the afternoon. Chandi was slightly put out, considering neither had consulted the pathfinder on her preference, but she understood. She went where she was needed and sometimes the need was greater than others.

While Chandi ran with Dora's sept, Ryland nursed his hangover and continued working with what he already had in addition to some mundane tools he had borrowed from Halldix's lab. He did as much prep work as possible before Chandi found him after lunch, ready for her second run of the day.

"This isn't going to be your normal meditation," he prefaced. "As a tinker-runner, there will be times when you are asked to procure certain components, so you need to know how to look for these things among the ruins. A lot of it is intuitive—if you are looking for wires, you want anything with electronics; if you are looking for medicine, you scan for red crosses or blue signs with a big H. Other times, it's less obvious and it comes down to reading the ruins and looking in the most probable place."

"So we aren't running so much as going on a scavenger hunt?" Chandi inquired.

Ryland wobbled his head ambivalently. "Well, you will still be meditating through motion, but think of it as passing your stillness through a tech filter." He let her review the list as he geared up, optimistically grabbing his large pack before they headed out. There was a lot of stop-and-goes as Ryland investigated promising sites and pointed out telltale signs to the pathfinder along the way. Toward the middle of the afternoon, he paused and quizzed her on what she saw. Chandi was accustomed to being aware of her surroundings—that was integral to finding the true path—but the wondrous potential of the ruins opened up once she knew what to look for.

Their packs were laden with parts when they returned an hour before dinner. Chandi dutifully helped unload and organize their finds by project so Ryland would be able to knock out as much work as possible the next day. Ryland set aside a few simple repairs that Chandi could work on in the afternoon, provided that Dora didn't require her. She returned to her room and put away the broken pocket watch she found, hoping she could fix it for her father in time for her impending visit.

As she readied for dinner, she hear someone approach her door. "I'll be there in a second, Willem," she called out as she splashed clean water on her face.

"It's not Willem," an amused tenor rumbled at her door.

Chandi grabbed a towel and dried her face. "Oh hey, Hendrix," she greeted the familiar face. "I was just on my way to dinner and thought you were Willem. Can I can help you with something?" She let down her hair and brushed it out.

He leaned against the doorframe. "I missed you at the lake this afternoon and wanted to make sure we didn't frighten you away."

Chandi let out a short laugh. "No, I don't scare that easy. I just had other things to take care of, and I fear my afternoons swimming the lake and sunning are over." She whipped her hair into a quick braid and pinned back the stragglers.

"That's a pity. Perhaps a swim after dinner?" he suggested with a twinkle in his eyes. "The lake is beautiful at night."

Chandi couldn't lie, it was tempting. Hendrix was incredibly good-looking and it would be an untruth if she said she didn't peek when he got out of the lake. "Isn't the water awfully cold at night?" she replied coyly.

"Well, we can do other things if you don't want to get cold and wet," he edged a little closer, giving her a mischievous grin.

"What did you have in mind?" Chandi flirted back.

"How about a moonlit stroll?" He shrugged his shoulders innocently. "It's supposed to be a full moon soon."

She tilted her head. "I do have a penchant for the moon."

Willem rounded the corner and almost collided into

Hendrix. "Sorry, didn't see you there! Chandi, you ready for dinner?"

"Yeah, just let me grab a sweater."

"I'll see you later, Chandi." Hendrix edged out of the room, leaving Willem with a puzzled look on his face.

"What's with you and Adonis?" Willem grilled her.

Chandi's brow wrinkled. "Since when do you know about Greek mythology?"

"I read," Willem objected. "Just kidding. Telly's nuts for Greek mythology and that's what he calls Hendrix behind his back, because he's incredibly good looking and knows it."

"That makes more sense," Chandi commented as she gathered her things and shooed Willem out the door.

"And you're dodging the question," he said accusatorially.

"Willem, you're my friend, not my chaperone," Chandi stated firmly. Willem had no rebuttal but kept his eye on them throughout dinner.

The shattered moon was bright and only partially hidden by cloud cover; its wavy reflection glistened in the water. "Did you know that the ancients used to believe the moon was made of cheese?" Chandi made conversation as she tried to skip another rock. This time, it bounced once before sinking into the dark waters.

"Huh, imagine how disappointed the first ancients that arrived on the moon must have been." Hendrix skimmed his rock across the water. Chandi lost count after six.

"This isn't your first time rock skipping, is it?" she wryly remarked.

He laughed. "Let's just say I had a misspent youth and spent a lot of time throwing things at the water when I wasn't in it."

Chandi launched another dud and groaned. "In my defense, I spent most of my youth in the church; there weren't many classes on skipping rocks."

He came up behind her and gave her another rock. "It's all in the wrist. You have to throw laterally so the trajectory of the rock goes across the surface of the water, not down into it." He held her wrist and flicked it out. "Like that."

Chandi mimicked his instruction and let the rock loose, bouncing three times before losing steam. "Well, if this pathfinder thing doesn't work out, you could totally become a skipping rock instructor," she joked as she turned around and found Hendrix's broad shoulders behind her. Her heart beat a little faster at his proximity and heat. She had to stop herself from reaching out and touching him, and instead looked up.

He bent his head down and kissed her. By all accounts, it was a good kiss—no gnashing of teeth, not too much tongue, not too wet, and no wide mouth that made her feel like he was trying to eat her face. Just a little pressure designed to draw her in. He was so close and warm and it was a fine kiss, so why was she analyzing it instead of enjoying it? Chandi's mind kept returning to the notion that it didn't feel right. She tried closing her eyes and getting into it, but it still felt wrong. Hendrix slid his arms around the small of her back and tried to deepen the kiss. It was flirtatious and sweet, but it wasn't Mika. Not that Mika and she were exclusive; they'd never even had that conversation. But there it was—a perfectly nice kiss from an incredibly attractive sentient in a romantic setting and she might as well have been kissing Willem.

Chandi placed her hand on his chest and pulled back. "That was nice, but not what I'm looking for."

"Oh," he uttered, and came on more aggressively.

"Nope, wrong direction." Chandi slipped out of his grasp, thankful for her training in Applied Tenets of Faith. He looked confused, and Chandi got the impression not many sentients told him no. "I'm sort of seeing someone and I thought it might be okay, but it's not. This isn't going to work for me. At all," she clarified with more words.

"Willem?" he guessed.

Chandi let out a short burst of laughter. "No, not Willem." She headed back toward the cloister house and called back when she noticed Hendrix wasn't following. "Are you coming?"

"I'm just going to go for a cold swim," he hollered back, taking off his clothes. His muscular form gleamed against the dark night, and Chandi watched him enter the water. The broken moon's reflection rippled from his strokes.

Chapter Thirteen

Chandi rose the next morning in high spirits—she was going to do her first bit of tinkering for tribute. Sure, that wasn't technically what she was sent here to do, but if something she repaired today was used in the cloister house, it counted in her mind. She was relieved when the morning passed without incident, despite the lack of late-night trysts at the lake, and the sept moved as one through the rituals and ruins.

When Chandi entered Ryland's makeshift workshop after lunch, he had already made a sizeable dent in the repairs but left one for her. She took her spot at the bench and went to work. According to her advisor, she had all the parts and tools to make it work; the rest was up to her.

She examined the broken tech, figuring out how the pieces were supposed to work in conjunction and to what end. From there, she could identify the part that wasn't working right and only then could she consider viable repair options. Could it be modified or would it need replacement? Was there more than one dysfunctional part? Was everything working properly but it lacked power? She muttered to herself and the pieces as she swapped tools, coaxing components to fit into place and behave.

After an hour, she loaded the batteries into the chamber and flicked the switch. A beam of light shot out the end, and Chandi swiveled it at her advisor. "Oh, you're finished!" Ryland exclaimed. "Let's take a look." He tested the on-off switch and unscrewed the casing to examine her work. "Nice work. I don't really have anything else for you to work on, but could you do me a favor and stop by Halldix's lab and pick up a flange wrench? I saw one hanging on his wall that I think will work on this stubborn connection." Ryland stared down the water pump as if it were a matter of pride at this point. "It's right next to where his old barracks were last fall."

"Flange wrench. Got it," Chandi confirmed before setting out. The cloister house was technically in the ruins, but it wasn't far from the nearby village or the octopoid's settlement. Chandi took a leisurely run and was awed at the difference a few months made. The fields were flowering and green, the trees were leaved, and the cold gloom of sickness no longer hung over the settlement. There were signs of recent repairs and renovations. The most notable were the additions to Halldix's quarters and the full-sized doors—a three-inch hole was fine for an octopoid but impractical for equipment and tech.

She knocked at the door and gave a formal bow when the king regent answered. "Your Tentacled Majesty, I come on behalf of Tracer Simons. He is in search of a flange wrench."

Halldix was delighted to see his healer and waved her inside. "I had no idea you were here. No one is sick, are they?"

"No, your highness. I'm here in a preventative capacity. Not all the dangers of the ruins come with teeth," Chandi replied.

He chuckled as he led her down the entryway. "By any chance, did you bring your pearl of making to Oswego?"

"Regretfully no. I carry a canteen when I travel and therefore use the freshwater pearl," Chandi respectfully fibbed.

Halldix waved a tentacle in a flippant gesture. "That's a pity. It was from my first batch and it would have been nice to see if it is consistent with the others of its array, for completeness's sake."

"Is there something wrong with the pearls of making?" Chandi politely inquired.

"Not exactly wrong. It's just that the second lot isn't nearly as nice and I was hoping to figure out why, especially since there were only eight in the first run." He opened another door and ushered her in.

As she passed the threshold, she was assaulted by parts, tools, and half-completed projects on every available surface and hanging from racks and wall pegs. The austerity of Ryland's workshop was the exact opposite of Halldix's. Halldix appraised Chandi's wandering eyes. "It's marvelous, isn't it?"

"Where did you find all this? I thought the Lordship of Fingers didn't venture into the ruins," Chandi asked in awe.

"In the water, naturally," he replied. "There are all sorts

of treasures to be found in the sea." It had never occurred to Chandi how much she was missing by not looking below the water's surface. "All life came from the water and all the wonders of Atlantis are still underwater, if the old tales are to be believed," he spoke as he combed the walls with six of his arms until he tracked down the desired tool. He used his suckers and prehensile limb to detach it from its hook. "Here you are, one flange wrench."

Halldix tracked Chandi's fixed gaze to the art adorning his wall. "Ah, that one was my uncle's favorite. He was obsessed with the old stories—the waters will rise and herald the rise of Atlantis! It's our version of Valhalla or heaven—a lovely fairy tale to tell the young." He stood beside the stunned pathfinder. "It's actually where I got my inspiration for the freshwater pearls and pearls of making," he added as he deposited the wrench into her hand. "Give Tracer Simons my regards and remind him to return this along with the others he borrowed before he leaves." There was a serious undertone to his jest.

"Of course, Your Tentacled Majesty. Thank you for your time," Chandi tumbled over her words as she tore her eyes from the tapestry—a gray pearl atop a gleaming fountain, just like she saw in her dream last fall, only this one was spewing forth copious water to the world below.

*****

Liam had been following Marbec all afternoon, giving him plenty of space to avoid detection. Liam was optimistic when Marbec wandered from his familiar haunts into what could only be considered the bad part of town—there were no salons or coffee houses in these tortuous lanes.

He watched from across the street as Marbec left an apothecary of questionable repute and waited a minute before entering. He slinked in through the entrance and requested for a rare concoction, something the apothecary would have to retrieve from the back. As the attendant rummaged through his inventory, Liam helped himself to the ledger, ascertaining what Marbec had purchased and how much.

Liam rotated the glass jars around until he found the right label—still on the counter from its recent sale. He liberated a healthy scoop onto a sheet of paper and folded it shut. Placing everything back as he found it, Liam exited the shop before the attendant returned.

It was a simple but effective plan. First, present a suggestion in such a way that it seemed innocuous enough to the morally hindered—the ends justify the means, and all that. Next, wait for them to act on the suggestion, using the smallest amount just to make the brood a little sick, nothing more. Then, administer the same substance at significantly greater amounts—the devil is in the dose.

When the brood died, Marbec would take the fall. With Droxithal's brood dead and Halldix discredited—he couldn't even keep his uncle's fry alive!—Lord Akkar could take the throne and Liam would ride the wave of his ascension. Liam knew his time was coming, he just had to be patient and stick to the plan.

*****

Chandi was quiet throughout dinner, but Flo needed no assistance to keep the conversation going. It had to be a coincidence. Of course the pearl of making looked like the image on the tapestry—the king regent admitted as much. Halfway through her now-cold stew, she pieced together an order of events from her memory—Halldix had just given her the pearl of making before she'd had that dream—that could easily explain its presence.

The only problem was that she couldn't explain the fountain. She could understand it showing up in her dream with the pearl, because they were both something she had experience with, but she couldn't explain why Emma's hedge maze fountain was in octopoid iconography. Maybe that just a classic look for a fountain—like when sentients heard "fountain," that's what they produced? Was it possible that she was misremembering and it wasn't the same fountain at all?

She muddled through the worst games of gin ever played as she processed everything she knew. There was no better scholar than Brother Bartholomew, Jackson had proven himself reliable time and time again, and she wouldn't have had made it through this past month without Ryland. She trusted her brothers of the stride, and if they told her nothing was wrong, that should be enough. Except that it wasn't.

Chandi excused herself from the others and took a stroll to the cloister house courtyard. She looked up at the moon. Tomorrow night, she would be back at Unseen Waters. She would retrieve her pearl from Jackson and get some answers, one way or another.

Willem took a seat next to her. "Hey, are you okay? You seem really distracted tonight."

"What? Yeah, I'm fine." Chandi smiled reassuringly. "Just thinking about all the things I have to do when I get back to the monastery."

Willem fished a letter. "Will you give this to Lucy for me?" Chandi secured it in her pocket. "Tell her I can't wait to see her in two weeks."

"Sure."

"And tell her I'm miss her so much, but don't make it sound like I'm completely miserable or she'll worry."

"Right, appropriately sad but not wretched."

"And tell her all the females are old and ugly, even the lay staff they bring in. She has nothing to worry about."

Chandi laughed—let it never be said Willem didn't know exactly who Lucy was. "I can do that."

"And that she's the best…" Willem tapered off.

"Okay, but I draw the line at making out with your girlfriend on your behalf," Chandi stated firmly.

Willem guffawed. "And you call yourself a true friend."

*****

A sharp knock rapped on the abbess's chamber door in the middle of the night. Khiri grabbed the robe beside her bed before answering. As soon as she saw the crest of the elder council on the messenger's tabard, she knew it was official business and it must be most pressing to send him at this time of night.

She broke the seal and pulled back the curtain to read the missive by the bright moonlight. It was only one sentence: *Be on alert for wave change.* Khiri scribbled a hasty reply to the council, requesting supplies and to broadcast a non-essential travel alert for Watertown. After the messenger left the monastery gates, the mother of the stride woke Ariadne. It was going to be a long night.

Chapter Fourteen

Once the communal stillness of morning devotion had been observed, the mother of the stride stepped off her dais to address the monastery at large. It was only a matter of time before the news came out—the staff, instructors, and administrators had already been briefed in the wee hours of the morning—and the abbess wanted to preempt rumors and panic. "If I could have your attention before we break for breakfast. Late last night, we received word from the main house. Unseen Waters is on alert for a wave change." A stunned hush broke the serenity they had just created.

"We have a protocol in place and are already making preparations, but the crucial points are as follows: I have issued a non-essential travel ban in and out of Unseen Waters effective immediately. Those already on route will complete their journey, but no new travel will begin. We will increase the frequency of morning devotion to three times a day and all pathfinders and tracers will engage in advanced ritual to bolster our position. The Order of the Guard will be moved inside the monastery walls; they are already at work converting the courtyard into a makeshift camp. There will be no patrolling or running of Watertown's ruins until the threat has passed. All meditations through movement will take place within the adaptive training ground and be on a reduced schedule to accommodate the previously mentioned changes." The abbess summoned her stillness against the rising anxiety that filled the room. "Otherwise, life will continue as usual. All this will be posted throughout the monastery's communal areas. Students, if you have questions, ask one of your instructors. Visitors, ask my prioress." The murmurs started as she came to her conclusion. The mother of the stride held up her hand and the room fell silent again. "Brothers and sisters of the stride, we will flow like water and ride this wave. Now go get some breakfast; we have a lot of work to do."

Everyone knew that the ruins changed; it was an accepted part of life under the shattered moon. There was some variation in scope and frequency depending on the ruins, but they were generally isolated changes—a new building here, a change in landscape there, maybe that rock shifted a few feet to the left or disappeared completely. After study and contemplation, the scholars and theologians determined these changes were actually small rips in time and space, which led the Church of Parkour to develop rituals to mitigate the occurrence and impact of changes—they literally reinforced and darned the tears in the fabric of reality with their directed communal will. The initial rituals anchored a place in space-time, keeping it firmly rooted in reality, granting the church unprecedented access to the ruins.

And then they experienced their first wave change—a tsunami of change that swept across a large swath of ruins. It didn't alter a few things here or there. It changed everything and decimated the Church of Parkour's installation in its path. In geology terms, if changes were small tremors, a wave change was "the big one." The scholars speculated that was how the ancient Greeks arrived in the Center Sea and formed the Thalassocracy of New Greece, and how the pyramids of ancient Egypt ended up in Memphis, Tennessee—they rode in during a wave change.

After the destruction of the Monastery of Bellevue, a collaborative effort between scholars and theologians made adjustments to the rituals and produced the wave change protocol. Instead of anchoring into space-time, they turned their focus on preserving their time and place to ride out the wave, turning the entire monastery and all its inhabitants into a lifeboat tethered to reality.

The monastery was a bevy of activity juxtaposed against the stillness found in continual ritual. A small section of the managed simulation zone was flattened for the tenderfoots and novices to train on while the pathfinders and tracers meditated in the more robust sections. The abbess knew the importance of meditation through movement, if for no other reason than to give their nervous energy focus and release, thus improving the caliber of their ritual stillness.

It was late afternoon when the carriage arrived from Oswego. The inhabitants knew something was wrong the second they saw the courtyard filled with the Order of the Guard. Ryland stepped out first to assess the situation, stopping a soldier pushing a handcart full of supplies. "What's going on?"

"We're barricading—a wave change is coming."

Ryland's face tightened. "Chandi, get inside."

*****

"Chandi, thank the founders you made it back!" Lucy embraced her roommate as she entered their room. "Did you hear? A wave change is coming."

"I heard." Chandi dropped her baggage. "When was it announced?"

"This morning." Lucy took a seat while Chandi unpacked. Suddenly the color drained from her freckled cheeks. "You don't think it could hit Oswego, do you?"

Chandi shook her head. "It's close, but not that close. If the main house thought they were in danger, they would have told them to come to Unseen Waters." Chandi dug into the pockets. "Speaking of which, I have a letter from Willem." Lucy clutched onto the slightly crumbled envelope.

"How is he?"

Chandi grinned. "He's in a good place for him to train,

but misses you terribly. So, all in all, it could be worse. He was planning to visit in two weeks, but I'm not sure how all this will effect that."

"And the lay of the land?" Lucy asked pointedly.

Chandi shook her head. "You don't have to worry about anything unless Willem has a thing for hot mermen."

Lucy's eyes lit up. "Do tell…"

"You're better off sticking with Willem. Not only are the goods bigger, they are always present," Chandi quipped. Lucy's eyes widened as she unpacked all that. "I'll tell you all about it but first, let me check in with Ryland and see what the abbess needs us to do."

Chandi roamed the hallways of the resident scholars and support staff until she found Ryland in Jackson's room. "Ah Chandi, I believe this belongs to you." The sorcerer deposited the pearl of making into her hands, glad to be rid of the tech. "As I anticipated, no spirit activity while you were gone."

Chandi performed a casual bow and tucked it into a pocket. "I was going to join the others in ritual, unless there is something else I should be doing." Neither of her brothers in stride had any better ideas, so the pathfinder took her leave.

The pathfinders, tracers, and scholars had taken over various classrooms for ritual meditation, rotating in shifts to give everyone a break to recuperate between stints. Chandi knew many of the rituals but some were new, only used in extreme circumstances. She assumed the position, found her stillness, and joined her brothers and sisters of the stride.

Chandi was uncertain how much time had passed, but came out of her meditations when someone touched her shoulder and took her place. She stood and stretched her limbs, and headed out for some dinner.

She grabbed a bowl of stew and found Sura, Hanu, and Lucy. Everyone was tired but glad to be in fellowship during these harrowing times. Chandi tried to lighten the mood with tales from Oswego, omitting any parts too personal or potentially distressing. They gaped at the idea of using lay staff to help with the upkeep of the premises. "What do they do with all that extra time?" Hanu marveled.

"Run and scavenge. They have quotas to make and tribute to pay," Chandi replied.

Sura shook her head and spoke with wisdom beyond her years, "They're gonna get you one way or another."

*****

Chandi ran to catch up with Sura after the last devotion of the night. "Hey Sura, do you have a moment? I need your help with something."

The blonde novice looked surprised but pleased. "Sure, what's up?"

Chandi found a quiet section of the commissary where the kitchen was putting out food and drink for the pathfinders and tracers that would perform rituals throughout the night. "Remember how you did that thing where you and I could talk without speaking?" Sura nodded. "Could you explain to me how you do it?"

Sura squished her face. "I've never really thought about it. It's just something I can do."

Chandi bobbed her head. "I get it. You do it without having to think about it, but maybe I could ask you some questions and break it down step by step?"

"Okay," the novice agreed. "If it would help."

"All right. So what do you do first, before you are connected?" Chandi prompted Sura.

"I usually ask if it's okay first and then I touch them. I've never tried to do it remotely or on someone that was unknowing," Sura qualified.

"This is good," Chandi encouraged her. "So you're touching them. Then what do you do? Are you thinking about anything? Saying any mantras?"

Sura concentrated. "Well, I picture myself and them in my head, only I'm in a bubble. Then I inflate my bubble until they are inside my bubble, too. Does that make sense?"

Chandi nodded. "Yeah, that makes sense. What do you do if you want to sever the connection?"

Sura answered like the answer was obvious, "I pop the bubble."

*****

Cabon couldn't shake the knot she had in her stomach after the meeting. It was one thing to grouse about your king regent's whims, it was another to suggest deliberately sickening the brood he was charged to bring into adulthood. Yakim did his best to brush the whole matter aside, but Cabon was unsettled nonetheless. She left her chambers and took a walk around the palace in hopes that checking on the fry would ease her mind.

As she came to the entrance of the royal pools, the overnight nanny was notably absent. Cabon called out and no one answered. She pushed the double doors open with two of her limbs and came upon the edge of the pool. It struck her as odd that the lights were turned off—fry this young still preferred some light at night.

She went to the wall and flipped the switch with her sucker and gasped at the handful of octopoids floating lifeless on the water's surface. Cabon reached for the strainer and edged the dead to the side. She focused on catching those still alive, relocating them to a smaller side pool. She switched on the filter and activated the pearl of making, rapidly turning over the water. She hoped she wasn't too late.

The remainder of Droxithal's brood were alive, if listless. Cabon hated to leave them, but she must send word to Halldix and there were few that she trusted with such an important task. She knocked on the wall of Erasmo's room, her cousin and broodmate, before sliding through the hole. He left at once with the message, and Cabon returned to the royal pool and started her vigil.

Chapter Fifteen

Chandi snuck down the hall and darted into Willem's unoccupied room—one of the benefits he retained by still being a tracer trainee. Ideally, she would try this outside under the blood moon, but with the entire Order of the Guard camped in the courtyard and the general hyperawareness of the entire monastery, this was going to have to do. The last thing she wanted was to be interrupted.

Chandi took a seat on Willem's made bed; she didn't know how long this was going to take and wanted a modicum of comfort. She reassured herself that, theoretically, it should work. It stood to reason that if Moonstone had no problem communicating with her directly once she was infested with nanites, she could be able to communicate with it now that she had better control over the nanites. All she had to do was initiate the conversation, and Sura was the only telepath she knew. She hoped that Sura's technique would work for her.

Chandi placed her pearl of making in her hand and assumed a meditative posture. She closed her eyes and summoned the stillness within. In her mind's eyes, she pictured herself and then Moonstone, picking a slightly less daunting figure but still a goddess—Chandi knew Moonstone well enough to know it took pride in its appearance. Chandi conjured a figure with milky skin draped in alabaster cloth. Her rich chestnut hair was bound back, affixed with a golden diadem that featured two crescents curled up in front. In her hand, she carried a lunar disk, wielding it like a scepter. Chandi conjured a bubble around her and slowly expanded its fluctuant borders. Each time she felt her nanites squirm, she redirect the energy into inflating her balloon a little more until it was just her and Moonstone.

The image in Chandi's mind took on a life of its own, examining its accoutrements. "You're going Greek?" Moonstone mused.

"I thought it was keeping in theme with the rise of Atlantis," Chandi wryly greeted her.

"I'm impressed—you really have mastered the black diamond. Communicating telepathically is not an easy feat," Moonstone complimented the pathfinder.

"This isn't exactly a social call," Chandi replied bluntly.

Moonstone, in the guise of Selene, pouted. "Well then, let's get down to business. What can I do for you?"

"Last time we spoke, you failed to mention your role in the rise of Atlantis," Chandi cautiously hedged her bets.

"Whatever do you mean?" the goddess feigned innocence.

"When I make you whole, you're going to produce enough

water to cover the whole planet. You didn't come to warn me about the apocalypse—you came to trick me into helping it come about!" Chandi cast her accusation.

"You mortals are such a bore! Does it even matter? A great flood here, a nuclear winter there, a plague of pestilence—one way of another, the cycle continues," Moonstone flippantly dismissed Chandi's anger. "Do you think this is the first time Atlantis has risen? I can't even count how many times I've watched from up there."

"So what, it's your turn to bring on the apocalypse? You guys draw lots, and you ended up with the short stick this time? Or is it some sort of honor among your kind?" Chandi retorted sarcastically.

All the gaiety drained from Moonstone's face, turning her beauty into sharp angles edged with shadows. "You think sentients are the only ones caught in a cycle of violence under the shattered moon? I have spent countless millennia waiting for the world to restart itself—waiting for the moon to be whole again—only to be sent to Earth, shattered into pieces like the moon itself, and imprisoned in a shell that severs any lunar connection I had."

"So it is you inside the pearl?" Chandi uttered with vindication.

"Why do you ask questions you already know the answer to?" Moonstone chided her. "I just want to be made whole before I must play my part in this farce." Moonstone had a look of pained longing.

Chandi softened her tone. "Do you *want* to bring on the rise of Atlantis?"

Moonstone stared, befuddled at the question. "What I want is immaterial. It will happen regardless if I'm here or not."

"What if I were to make you whole and *you* went to the alternate time?" Chandi proposed. "Before the moon was shattered, the science of the ancients still reigned—you could be free of this monstrous form thrust upon you, free of both sorcery and super science."

Moonstone eyed Chandi with grave intent. "It will not stop the waters from rising, only delay it. Another will take my place."

"Sure, but it doesn't have to be now and it certainly doesn't have to be you," Chandi pointed out, hoping such things mattered to Moonstone.

Moonstone-as-Selene tilted her delicate head. "Only one of us can go through. Are you sure you're willing to give up your escape? Isn't that what you're training for?"

"I'll have time to find another way if you go through now," Chandi reasoned.

Moonstone folded her arms and shifted in her toga. "I'm curious, how do you know that I will keep my end of the bargain once I am made whole? That I'm not some anathema of magic and technology?"

"I don't," Chandi answered. "But I know how much this

form pains you. I don't remember how many times I've been through the cycle of reincarnation, but you can remember every second since the beginning. You have seen it all, and you will exist forever to see it happen over and over again. Do you really want to spend the rest of eternity under the shattered moon in this state? What I am offering is nothing less than peace—a place where the real moon is whole, not just an illusion you created to soothe yourself. A place where they still celebrate the harvest moon. I have to think that is an offer you would take."

Moonstone considered her words for some time before the corners of her mouth upturned. "I see now why the black diamond chose you. I agree to your terms."

"Good," Chandi responded. "Now, tell me how to make you whole again."

*****

The first mound of tribute was carted into Halldix's lab last night; what others called junk, a tinker saw as opportunity. He was fiddling with the remains of a portable cassette player when he heard a ruckus at his front door. He made his way outside where two members of his octopoid militia were trying to discern what a third octopoid wanted. He didn't recognize Erasmo at first, but once he flashed his colors to the guards, Halldix told them to stand down and ushered his old friend in—Erasmo was pugnacious in the best of times. His unexpected visitor was still wet from his swim and didn't waste time.

"Cabon sent me with word that someone has poisoned the brood. She has saved those that she could, but some have already perished. You must come with me to Syracuse immediately and put an end to the madness!"

Ire rose in Halldix—who would stoop so low to attack fry? He didn't know, but he was going to find out. He donned his girdle of power and ordered his faithful octopoid militia to ready for an immediate departure.

As he gathered his things, Cassie entered his open front door with the intent of seeing how Halldix found his first tribute. It didn't take long for the sorcerer to gather that all was not well. "Your Tentacled Majesty, is something wrong?" She bowed and addressed him formally in the presence of the octopoid unknown to her.

"Treachery in Syracuse! Someone has poisoned my uncle's brood. I must return immediately," Halldix fumed. "Do you think you could get your healer to Syracuse? Some have already died, and I fear the worst by the time I arrive."

She did some rough calculations. "If we had a fresh change of horses, we could arrive sometime tomorrow if I leave immediately. Would Your Tentacled Majesty find that pleasing?" Something in Cassie's voice prompted Halldix to face her and see the unspoken meaning in her eyes.

"Yes, Sister Cassandra. I welcome you and the healer of

the Church of Parkour to the royal palace in Syracuse for the purpose of aiding the poisoned brood," Halldix proclaimed for the benefit of Erasmo and the octopoid militia. "If your healer will bring her pearl of making and show it to the octopoid militia, they will know you two as friends and direct you to me."

Cassie gave a formal bow. "As you wish, Your Tentacled Majesty." She raced back to the cloister house, collecting her thoughts. Her first concern was Halldix—a kingdom hardly needs a king regent if there are no offspring to raise to adulthood. She'd put too much work into this relationship to have it not pan out now. Dora was still out with the sept, and there was no time to waste. The sorcerer instructed the carriage to be readied, hastily assembled her travel gear, and scrawled a note for the sept leader.

She should arrive at Unseen Waters by late afternoon, and it would take some time to convince Khiri and Chandi of the gravity of the situation. If they left immediately, they risked traveling at night but would arrive in Syracuse the following morning. Alternately, they could wait until early morning and arrive that evening. Cassie knew from experience that a few hours could be the difference in Halldix retaining his station and being overthrown, depending on how the situation was handled. She bade the driver to push faster—they could always swap out horses at the monastery.

She reviewed the notes she had taken during her evenings

with Halldix: names, places, connections, grievances, gossip—anything that could give her an edge while she was inside the Lordship of Fingers' capital. The hardest part was going to be putting faces to the names; call her speciest, but all octopoids looked alike to her. She knew Halldix, but that was one individual; the ins and outs of features that distinguished one octopoid from another was a whole other matter. She was fine as long as they socially broadcast in a consistent manner—she could memorize coloring and patterns or insignias marking station—but it didn't help that octopoids often didn't wear clothing and had the ability to change both the color and pattern of their skin at the drop of a hat. She rued the fact that she couldn't put nametags on them.

Nothing seemed amiss at first, but as Cassie's carriage neared the monastery, she knew something was wrong—the flag of the Order of the Guard was not flying from their barracks and the gates were closed in the middle of the day. Cassie cursed her luck; last winter, she came right before a wastelander attack; founders only knew what she was walking into now.

She steadied her mind and called out to the otherworld, seeing if they could give her any insight. Cassie's brow furrowed—the closer she got, the fewer voices in her head. The sorcerer didn't know what was happening at Unseen Waters, but she was determined to get in, get what she needed, and get out.

Chapter Sixteen

Chandi felt a tap on her shoulder and broke her mantra. It didn't seem like she had been sitting long, but sometimes it was hard to tell in the depths of meditation. Ariadne's cluster of eyes greeted her as the prioress motioned for her to follow. Once they were in the hallway, she hustled Chandi toward the abbess's office, her legs tapping a rapid staccato on the monastery's floors.

Chandi entered and saw Khiri pacing and Cassie sitting on the edge of her seat. They both turned their attention to the pathfinder. "Please take a seat, Chandi. Sister Cassandra has a proposition for you. It is your decision to make according to your agreement with the church," the mother of the stride stated deliberately, subtly reminding Chandi of her right to refuse given the circumstances.

Cassie stood and made her case. "We received an urgent message in Oswego this morning: someone has poisoned the young in Syracuse. His Tentacled Majesty races to his capital as we speak, but before he left, he specifically asked for you to attend to his uncle's ailing brood. It is both a great honor and compliment as we would be the first sentient vertebrates invited into the capital of the Lordship of Fingers, and your healing ability could be the ambassador that brings closer relations with the octopoids. Will you come with me and heal his wards?"

Chandi answered without skipping a beat. "Of course, I go where I'm needed." Cassie breathed a sigh of relief. "I just need to gather my things and let my roommate know. We can leave in thirty minutes?"

Cassie nodded, thankful Chandi understood that time was of the essence. "That will be fine—just enough time to change out for fresh horses and gather provisions from the kitchen. Don't forget to bring your pearl of making—that's how the octopoid militia are going to identify us as friends and safely deliver us to His Tentacled Majesty when we arrive." Chandi bowed before leaving the room and left her sisters of the stride.

Khiri waited until Chandi closed the door before she railed into Cassie. "That was a low, appealing to her better nature. You made it sound like a save-the-children mission!"

"You started it! You opened with 'you know you can say no,'" Cassie mimicked her old friend.

"Both of you are mad, traveling when there is a wave change coming!"

"Are you kidding?" Cassie scoffed. "Getting out of Watertown before it hits is the sanest thing I've heard of. If there were crickets in the otherworld, you could hear them out there because there are no voices. No. Voices. Khiri."

Khiri hated to admit Cassie had a point. Instead she moderated her tone; if these were the last words she said to Cassie, she didn't want them to be heated. "If this is a coup attempt and it goes bad, I want you two to run. No heroics, no sacrificial lambs, no scheming to save it—just get the hell out of octopoid territory and pull your Oswego sept to Unseen Waters, wave change or not."

Cassie gave Khiri a hug. "I promise I'll get her out if it goes bad." Khiri returned the embrace. "We are sisters of the stride. If there is one thing we know how to do, it's run." A short laugh bubbled from the tigress's tight chest.

"I can give you one squad of the Order of the Guard as protection. It's all I can spare in case…" Khiri's words tapered off; she didn't want to finish the sentence or the thought.

"You are Khiri Tham, tracer of the true path and mother of the stride of Unseen Waters. If anyone can lead this monastery safely through the storm, it's you."

*****

"You're leaving? In the middle of a wave change alert?" Lucy reiterated, just to be clear she understood her roommate.

Chandi threw her stuff in her pack, triple checking that she had both her freshwater pearl and her pearl of making. "I don't have time to go into all of it, but it's something I have to do,

Lucy. Trust me, if it wasn't absolutely necessary, I wouldn't be going."

"Why does it always have to be you? Can't someone else go on these crazy, last minute, spur-of-the-moment missions? Can't they just need you to stay put and help protect the monastery?" Lucy started crying. "Willem's out there and now you, too…what happens if I lose both of you? And I'm not talking about 'we're growing up and going our separate ways' but 'sorry, you're ripped out of space-time now.'"

Chandi dropped her bag on her bed and took Lucy in her arms. "I don't know if everything is going to turn out okay, but I do know that I will do everything I can to get back here. No wave change is going to alter that. And if by some turn of fate, I don't come back, it is against my will and I will go down fighting." Chandi rubbed Lucy's back the same way Mika did when she was upset. "I don't want to freak you out, but I need you to do me a favor. If I don't come back, can you tell Mika how much he meant to me? Everyone else here knows, but I never got the chance to tell him."

"How am I not supposed to freak out now?!" she blubbered harder.

"Lucy?" Chandi spoke firmly but tenderly.

"Yes, of course I will."

"And I promise *when* I come back, I will tell you absolutely everything."

"Even the super-secret stuff you're not supposed to tell

me?"

"Every last tidbit."

Lucy dried her eyes. "Come on, you're going to miss your ride."

*****

In the fading daylight, Halldix marched into Syracuse with his octopoid militia and let himself be seen, standing tall on his legs with the girdle of power fastened high under his visceral hump and a cascade of lights flowing down his body. Nothing spoke to the octopoids like pageantry. He burst into the palace and went straight to the royal pool to check on his uncle's brood. His three hearts were saddened to see their numbers halved.

Cabon bowed and greeted her lord. "I tried to save as many as I could," she apologized. "One in ten were already dead when I found them last night. I moved them to the smaller side pool, turning over the fresh water as quickly as possible to try and flush the poison. The rest have passed in clusters throughout the day."

"Cabon, my faithful advisor, without your quick thinking, they might have all been lost. Do you have any idea who could have done this?"

Cabon wailed with the guilt that had settled on her during her vigil, made heavier with each dead fry she pulled from the surface. "If only I had contacted you sooner…"

Halldix placed a tentacle on the side of her visceral hump and applied slight suction, a gesture of tenderness. "Start from the beginning and tell me everything."

Cabon unburdened herself, telling her lord about the conversation among his advisors. "It was crazy talk! It must have been a mistake. One of the others must have put something in the royal pool and used too much on accident. Or maybe they used something that only sickens adults but is particularly deadly to fry."

Halldix paced the floor. "And you haven't flushed the royal pool?"

"No, Your Tentacled Majesty. I was going to but I thought you would want to examine it," Cabon replied.

"You thought correctly. Now that I have returned, I will post the octopoid militia here. Get some rest. You have done well," he bolstered his steadfast advisor. She clutched two of her tentacles in front of her and left her king.

Halldix opened his case and carefully collected numerous samples of the water from the royal pool as well as the bodies collected in a bucket against the wall. He considered Cabon's scenarios but added another to her list: someone was making a grab for the throne and the fastest way was assassinating Droxithal's brood.

He would run tests and investigate. When he found those responsible, he would punish them in the old way—let them never say he was unoctopoid again. The last thing he did before he left the guards was turn on the water filter in the royal pool to high and activate all the pearls of making he had, diluting the filth that had killed his kin.

*****

Jackson stood on the monastery wall and watched the lightning storm in the distance. The branches of electricity lit up the night sky. Thirty minutes earlier, it had been snowing, and before that, rain with hail. Even the weather didn't know what time it was. The night was quiet, even to his sorcerous senses.

After the initial shock, it was kind of nice not hearing the voices of the otherworld; despite decades of practice, it still took a modicum of effort to filter and block out the noise in order to function in the real world. Additionally, there wasn't much for a sorcerer to do in the face of a wave change except prepare to clean up the spirits after the wave broke. For the first time in his four-plus decades, he had the luxury to turn philosophic. It was novel at first, but philosophy was like liquor—a little can lift your mood but too much makes you miserable, and it's a fine line between the two.

Ryland climbed up and put a thermos of warm coffee between them. The tinker-runner pulled out his binoculars, taking a closer look at the ruins. The edge of the storm was a few miles away, but if he fixed his vision on one spot, he could see the skyline morph as buildings disappeared and new ones materialized—all in a state of decay. They called them "ruins" for a reason.

Jackson popped the seal and poured the steaming brown sludge into his cup. "Still think I'm paranoid?"

Ryland kept his eyes on the horizon. "Just because something is coming after you doesn't mean you're not paranoid."

The sorcerer took a sip of his black coffee as another arc of lightning streaked down. "Touché."

*****

Cassie drifted in and out of sleep as the carriage rocked back and forth on the remains of the ancients' road. Each time she woke, she instinctively assessed her surroundings and found Chandi sleeping across from her. Cassie initially insisted her restlessness was a reaction to Chandi's nanites—the sorcerer had trained herself to become accustomed to nanites in the time she had spent with Halldix, but when she was asleep, her unconscious mind reigned. However, as the night progressed, it grew into a pang of conscience.

Cassie watched Chandi and recalled there was a time when she could fall asleep at a moment's notice anywhere. The pathfinder was just at the beginning of everything, and Cassie had made Khiri a promise that Chandi's journey wouldn't end in the Lordship of Fingers. Cassie knew what she was getting into but after a few hours of mulling, she was willing to admit that she hadn't exactly given Chandi the whole story. It wasn't that Cassie lacked scruples, she just had an explicit understanding that she was right; if everyone else understood that, she wouldn't have to go to the lengths she did to accomplish what was necessary.

The sun was starting to rise when Cassie gently shook Chandi awake. "We're almost there." The pathfinder rubbed the sleep from her eyes and worked out the kink in her neck from leaning against the side of the cab.

"Did you get any sleep?" Chandi inquired.

"I'll be fine," Cassie reassured her. "I want to talk to you about what we are walking into." She was careful with her words. "Not all octopoids are like His Tentacled Majesty— he is a very open-minded, scientific thinker that welcomes interaction with other types of sentients. That won't be the case in Syracuse."

"How so?" Chandi inquired.

"Most of the octopoids in the Lordship of Fingers have only ever been around other octopoids. Some may be like him but will be initially cautious or suspicious because they don't know any better. Everything we think of as normal—the way we move, talk, dress, eat—will seem weird to them and vice versa. You may even have some octopoids refuse to acknowledge your presence or actively insult you. Don't ask me why, but their favorite insult is that we have spines." Cassie rolled her eyes in an uncharacteristically unguarded moment.

Cassie gathered her composure again. "I need you to rise above all that because once we enter Syracuse, you are a representative of the Church of Parkour, just like me. We both have to show them the best the church has to offer. We have to be above reproach in all ways. Do you understand?"

Chandi nodded, feeling the weight of her decision.

"Good. Just follow my lead, bow when I bow, and always address everyone formally. Get your pearl ready; I see the checkpoint ahead. And remember, you were invited to be here. You belong here. Don't let any eight-limbed sentient tell you otherwise. Just because we are humble, doesn't mean we can't stand tall." Cassie took a deep breath in and put on her game face. Chandi observed and mimicked her posture.

The carriage slowed, and there was a tense moment where the octopoid militia and Order of the Guard sized up one another. Eventually, a tentacle knocked on the door. Cassie drew back the curtain and announced in a clear voice. "Sister Cassandra, sorcerous advisor of the elder council and Pathfinder Choudary, healer of the Church of Parkour are here by request of His Tentacled Majesty Halldix Kepoi. Know that we are friends of the octopoids." Chandi formally nodded and held up the pearl of making. The guard waved the carriage through. Cassie sat tall and left the curtain open for all of Syracuse to see.

Chapter Seventeen

The events of the past forty-eight hours had rocked Syracuse, and the rumors were flying. As if the news of the dead fry wasn't shocking enough, to learn that it was poison was simply unfathomable. Even if the circumstances were regrettable, the sudden return of His Tentacled Majesty in his regalia and with his show of strength was a welcomed sight and stilled their triple hearts, only to be stunned at the news of vertebrates in Syracuse, escorted by the octopoid militia to the royal palace. The residents of northern Syracuse lined the streets to catch a glimpse. The consensus was that they were gangly looking things, rigid and hairy.

The royal palace was the refurbished remains of a yacht club whose proximity to the water and distance from the actual ruins of Syracuse made it ideal for the octopoids. Each of the noble houses claimed a section of the interior, which had plenty of meeting rooms and offices to suit their needs, although many of the doorways were boarded and replaced with octopoid entrances: holes three inches in diameter, roughly two feet off the ground. The repair of the lights and mechanics of the indoor pool was one of the first tinkering feats that brought a younger Halldix a measure of cachet. Designated as the royal pool, it became the private domain of His Tentacled Majesty and a sacred place for the mating ritual and brooding chamber.

Halldix greeted his guests and hastily directed Chandi to the royal pool. Fortune smiled on them as the doors remained intact, albeit rarely used. A wave of nausea hit Chandi as the guard opened the door—whatever was used still lingered. Chandi did her best to maintain her composure. "Your Tentacled Majesty, the pool needs to be drained and scrubbed to remove the poison. It's quite overpowering." Cassie offered the pathfinder her arm, and they proceeded to the separate pool tucked into a nook. The fry were tightly constricted in such a small space, and Halldix was anxious to get them back into the larger royal pool—but not before he knew it was safe. Thankfully, there were no more floating on the top of the water.

A flurry of activity started once Halldix flashed lights and colors along his body, and an army of suckered limbs holding brushes and brooms started on the walls as the water level descended. Halldix turned his attention to Chandi, who had already dropped her pack and started undressing. She lowered herself into the water and found a built-in seat that was the right height to keep her head and shoulders dry. The listless juvenile octopoids scurried at the break in the water, but as it settled, they spread out once more. Chandi started singing aloud, resisting the urge to vomit. Halldix ordered the guards to protect the brood and the Church of Parkour's healer before taking his leave with Cassie.

Cassie quietly followed Halldix to his chambers, ignoring the gaping stares of the octopoid intelligentsia—of all his subjects, their curiosity overcame their fear the fastest. He walked tall and with purpose, as if he were puffing out his chest...if he had a chest. She remained silent as Halldix closed the squeaky door behind them and plugged the octopoid entrance—he was taking extra precautions in light of recent events. Only then did he drop his pomp.

"It was definitely poison, bad enough to elicit such a response in Chandi. What have you discovered?" Cassie queried Halldix.

"Two nights ago, both night nannies were told they had the night off, leaving the brood unattended. The last octopoid to see them uninjured was around dinnertime. My trusted advisor Cabon found them around two in the morning, and that's when she sent her cousin Erasmo to Oswego—someone she knew I would trust. I have identified the substance used, and the octopoid guards are checking the apothecaries and chemists for recent purchases, but that is as far as I've gotten."

He paced to his makeshift lab. "I do know that this was no accident. This was a deliberate attempt to kill the brood. The concentration of poison in the water samples I took is way too high to be a mistake. If Cabon hadn't checked on the brood in the middle of the night, they would have all been dead by the morning."

Halldix took a seat and sagged under the weight of his burden. "This is all my fault, Cassie." He made a gesture with four of his limbs that Cassie came to understand as resigned culpability. "If I were a better king regent, a better octopoid, this wouldn't have happened."

Cassie sat beside him and took one of his tentacles into her palm and stroked the back. "Or, some eight-armed asshole attacked defenseless juveniles and you came back in time before they could finish the job." Halldix applied slight suction to her hand. "Chandi is with them now. She has taken sickness from you, she has taken sickness from me. She will do her best to take the poison from your uncle's fry," Cassie reassured him.

*****

After a few hours, Chandi's stomach settled to the point where she could entertain the notion of food. She was relieved when Cassie brought her a sandwich and some fruit—she was not up for exotic foods or the social minefield of a diplomatic meal. Chandi left the water and wrapped herself with the towel she so wisely brought from the monastery before nibbling on some bread. Both the sisters of the stride were acutely aware of the octopoid guards in their presence and spoke cautiously.

"Do they know who did this?" Chandi inquired, saying more with her eyes.

"Not yet, but I have every faith that His Tentacled Majesty will get to the bottom of it." Cassie nodded suggestively. "Your job is the stay with the brood. You let me take care of the rest."

"They are almost done scrubbing the pool and will start refilling it shortly. The brood should be able to be moved by this evening. They will want to spread out once they start feeling better," Chandi observed. "Would it be possible to get a cot and blanket here instead of staying in one of the guest rooms? Maybe put a curtain across this nook for privacy? That way I could stay close to the brood but the octopoid guards can remain on watch through the night." Chandi raised one of her eyebrows.

Cassie appreciated her understanding of "above suspicion." "I think that sounds like a noble idea, but I must check with His Tentacled Majesty."

"You may want to let someone know to bring some food for the brood. They aren't biting, but they are starting to taste me with their suckers," Chandi added.

"They're hungry—that's a good sign!" Cassie spoke extra loud for the benefit of the guards. "I'll see what I can do, but if the worst of it has passed, perhaps you can stay out of the water until after they have eaten."

*****

Liam didn't know how the plan had failed, but each

day brought more bad news. Liam's expression of shock was genuine when he heard only half of the brood was dead the morning after his visit to the royal pool. As soon as Liam heard of the king regent's sudden return, he feared the worst. Under Lord Akkar's watch, there would have been the appearance of an investigation, but Halldix wouldn't stop until he found who murdered Droxithal's fry. Liam had one thing right—Halldix loved his uncle.

He did not dare to administer more poison and risk Halldix's faithful octopoid militia. Liam had one last hope: the rest of the brood would surely die soon and Lord Akkar would take the throne by popular opinion. That would put a halt to any investigations Halldix had in place. He spent a fretful night praying for death only to hear there were vertebrates in Syracuse. Gossip trickled out of the royal pool: a healer from the Church of Parkour!

Liam knew his time was up and made hasty plans to flee before retribution caught up with him. The octopoid was about to slide through his door when a cascade of tentacles tumbled into his room. The four octopoid militiamen proceeded to seize the advisor, and his tentacles were no match for their genetically bred strength.

Halldix entered the room, his bulk expanded by his righteous outrage. Liam quivered and begged for mercy. "Like the mercy you showed Droxithal's fry?!" Halldix's words pierced Liam's three hearts, for even he knew he was unworthy of grace.

"You have murdered my kin. For that you must die, but how you die is up to you." Halldix paced the room with his girdle of power held high. "It was clever setting up Marbec to take the blame, but doubly treacherous. Give me the name of your collaborators, and I will spare you death by sunning." Liam shuttered at the thought—each tentacle staked to the ground and baked in the dry heat of the infrared sauna.

Liam's visceral head dropped in defeat. "Lord Akkar."

"Is that all?" Halldix interrogated him.

"Yes, my lord."

Halldix put five vials of water on the table beside Liam's bed. "You will die as you have killed." With justice dispensed, His Tentacled Majesty exited the room. The four members of the octopoid militia surrounded Liam, waiting for it to be done.

*****

Chandi glided through the fresh water of the royal pool, swimming playfully with the fry. They were amused at her ineffectual strokes and applied a suction with their small cups on her leg in an aquatic form of tag. They tired quickly but Chandi took comfort that they were eating, swimming, and playing. Halldix was pleased to see the brood's improvement and left them to their games.

Chandi finished her last stint in the royal pool and swiped

the last large pearl of making, concealed from the guards in the exaggerated act of toweling off. Halldix had put all his pearls of making into use to fill the pool so quickly, and Chandi had been systematically taking one of the larger ones each time she exited the water. It had taken all day, but if her mental count was right, she should have all eight.

She retreated to her cot in the small alcove and pulled the curtain for privacy. She deposited the last gray pearl into her pack, dressed, and waited for the lights to dim, signaling bedtime for the fry. She had to be by water, and she hoped the smaller pool would be large enough—she had never opened a rift into an alternate timeline before.

Chandi sat on the edge of the water and assumed a meditative position. She held a pearl of making in each hand and concentrated, directing her will and her nanites. She brought her hands together and fused the two pearls into one slightly bigger pearl. Her heart beat fast as she added another and another. As the gray pearl grew larger, it became easier to accrete, like two magnets drawn to each other. She continued silently through the night until only her pearl of making stood separate, saving it for last.

Chandi withdrew it from her pocket and hesitated. If she had somehow gotten it terribly wrong, this could be the beginning of the rise of Atlantis. She didn't know if she could trust Moonstone to keep its word, but she felt fairly certain she could count on its own selfish desires. Chandi took a deep breath and pressed in her pearl of making. There were no big bangs or a flood of water, just a soft warm glow from within the giant gray pearl, now the size of a small apple.

Chandi touched the bottom of the pearl to the surface and the water started to swirl, spinning faster and tighter into a whirlpool that reached impossible depths well beyond the bottom of the pool that had held all the surviving fry just hours earlier. *May you find the stillness you seek*, Chandi bid Moonstone before she released the pearl and watched its light sink into the vortex. After it disappeared into the depths, the water finally stilled.

Chapter Eighteen

Everyone could feel the ripping of space-time occurring all around the monastery as they gathered in the main hall to ride out the wave. The past two days were spent gluing together the reality within the monastery walls, but now was the time of testing. Their tether to reality must hold or all could be lost.

The mother of the stride sat on her dais and led the entire monastery through the litany of stillness. The incense was thick from hours of meditation, and the prayer wheel was spun countless times. Khiri felt the metaphysical push and pull of the oncoming wave and began the ritual of the green reed as the winds beat down on all sides. She voiced the mantra aloud for the benefit of those not skilled in advanced ritual. Her voice droned against the rattle of the prayer wheel, and the brothers and sisters of the stride joined their voices and will. "The green reed that bends in the wind is stronger than the mighty oak that breaks in a storm."

Khiri felt the surge pull on their tether, stretching it to its limits, but it did not break. A rolling tide of pressure passed over Unseen Waters, jarring those inside, but the ritual continued.

The abbess continued even though the winds and the pressure subsided, ever vigilant for aftershocks. They were small and barely perceptible compared to the zenith of the crashing wave.

The mother of the stride felt a hand on her shoulder, insistently shaking her, but she was unyielding in her devotion: the tether must hold. Then a voice whispered into her ear. She recognized Jackson's baritone. "Abbess, the voices are back." Khiri brought the Monastery of Unseen Waters out of ritual and back to reality, and only then did she break her concentration to thank the founders.

*****

Halldix leaned back and let his limbs relax. What remained of the brood was safe and on the mend, he had administered justice to the responsible parties, and he was wrapped around his favorite vertebrate. They lounged together in repose, enjoying a private moment out from under the watchful eye of Syracuse.

"I have to stay, Cassie," he stated matter-of-factly.

"I know," she replied.

"I have enjoyed our time together," he added wistfully.

"You make it sound so final. It's just for a little while. Once your uncle's brood are adults, you can leave Syracuse again," she remarked.

"It will be years until one of them ascends the throne, and

by that time, I will be expected to breed. And die." Halldix flashed a deep green at the tip of his tentacles, which Cassie understood as a sign of regret or apology.

The sorcerer shook her head. "No, that's unacceptable."

"Cassie, there is no other way," he insisted. "I have a duty to fulfill, and the last time I shirked it, my uncle's brood almost died."

The gears were already turning in her mind. "What if you were to hold court in Oswego for a season and bring the brood, maybe in the summer when the waters are at their warmest?" she suggested.

"I go to Oswego to escape Syracuse. Why would I bring Syracuse with me to Oswego?" he mused. He tasted her skin, an earthy saltiness he had come to appreciate.

Cassie's mind flipped to advisor-mode. "It would allow you to normalize relations between octopoids and vertebrates, making any subsequent visits to Oswego a part of official royal business instead of a scandalous escapade. If the brood has regular interactions with vertebrates, they are more likely to continue in the progressive direction you envision for the Lordship of Fingers. And it's a good way to weed out undesirable advisors—anyone that is dead-set against spending a couple of months in Oswego swimming in Lake Ontario is not someone you want giving you advice."

Halldix considered her idea…after all, he did need two new advisors. "This summer is out of the question. There is too much planning and construction involved to set up court. It would have to be next summer."

"If you can't come to Oswego, maybe I can come to Syracuse," Cassie asserted coquettishly.

"Cassie, what do you have up your sleeve?" Halldix was slowly picking up on vertebrate sayings.

"What if I told you that the Church of Parkour has been asked by the Kingdom of a Thousand Islands to mediate peace with the Lordship of Fingers?" Her eyes gleamed while Halldix did the octopoid equivalent of raising an eyebrow. "The new monarchs want to break with their old ways to steer their kingdom in a different direction. Sound familiar?" she teased. "I could send an official letter in a month or two—enough time for you to secure your position here—and we could start discussing terms. There are a lot of details to work out: borders, movement of sentients, trade deals. It could take months of extensive negotiations to come to an agreement."

He wrapped around her a little tighter. "Do you always get what you want?"

Cassie smiled. "Only if I really want it."

*****

A catharsis passed over Syracuse once the conspirators were punished and the procession of the dead commenced. The octopoids wailed and flashed their colors during the death rite for Droxithal's fry. Because their flesh retained the poison, they could not follow tradition and be fed to the remaining brood. In his infinite ingenuity, His Tentacled Majesty borrowed a rite from the vertebrate and immolated their bodies. The consensus was that the old ways were best but sometimes needs must.

Cassie, Chandi, and the Order of the Guard stayed away from the funeral out of respect for the Lordship of Fingers; it had been a trying time for their community. Even though they were conspicuously absent, the vertebrates were on everyone's mind. What was the world coming to when octopoids poison octopoids and a vertebrate must come to heal them?

Halldix was still trying to uncover the mystery of what had happened to his first batch of pearls of making, which had disappeared overnight from the royal pool. When asked, Chandi reported that hers was missing, too; it had been in her pocket but she was in and out of her clothing so much swimming with the fry, it was impossible for her to know when it went missing. The guards swore that no one unauthorized entered the royal pool, and Chandi was either with the fry or on her side of the curtain the entire time. An extensive search of her possessions and the area yielded nothing.

When Halldix offered to give Chandi another pearl of making from the second batch to replace the purloined one, she politely declined—it wouldn't be the same and she didn't come here to be rewarded. She was a pathfinder of the Church of Parkour; she went where she was needed.

Cassie and Chandi returned to the cloister house, anxiously waiting to hear news from the monastery. Chandi fell into their routine, processing what had transpired in Syracuse. There was definitely a sense of loss, like she was missing some part of her, but she was also heartened. Perhaps it was a part of her that was best left excised. Maybe Mika was right: some relationships were better left in the past.

After a few days, news came out of Unseen Waters: it still stood, albeit in a changed Watertown. The abbess put out a call for all available runners to assist in remapping the area with sorcerous and tech support as well as regular Order of the Guard patrols. Cassie accompanied Willem and Chandi back to the monastery and left Dora in charge of the cloister house. The first tribute had already been delivered and with Chandi's extra help scavenging, they were ahead enough on the next tribute to afford to pitch in with the relief effort.

As they approached the monastery, Chandi looked out the window with wonder—the ruins were completely different than when she left a mere week ago. They were still rubble of the ancients, but no one knew what treasures and dangers they held or from what time they had been ripped. Even though they were entering a new Watertown, the walls of Unseen Waters stood unchanged and the Church of Parkour flag proudly flew from its heights.

The abbess greeted the carriage as it entered the courtyard. Willem and Chandi bowed to the mother of the stride, who welcomed them home with a bow and released them to find their friends. Khiri and Cassie watched them swerve through the bustle of activity as the Order of the Guard disassembled their camp and moved into their new barracks, recently cleared by Ryland as structurally sound, but only after Jackson had declared it free of unwanted spiritual guests.

"All is well in Syracuse?" Khiri politely inquired as they entered the monastery.

"Those responsible have been punished. The octopoids will have to find their own peace with that," Cassie answered. "She looks good, Khiri. I don't even see a stone misplaced."

"We flow like water over the land," the mother of the stride replied modestly.

Cassie subtly smiled. "You need an extra sorcerer? I may not be a pathfinder or a tracer, but I came ready to bag some spirits," she offered, polishing her lapis lazuli pendant.

"I'm sure we can find something to keep you busy; I have it on good authority that the voices of the otherworld are back."

*****

"You're not dead!" Lucy squealed when Chandi opened the door to their room, and bear hugged her. Chandi let herself be crushed. "Have you seen it out there? It's completely different. Even the Order of the Guard barracks are changed—now it's red brick and two stories with a staircase and a pole. And that's literally right next to the monastery."

"Yeah, it looked totally different than when I left. I guess I'll have plenty of interesting running in my future."

Lucy pointed a sharp finger at Chandi's chest. "You have a lot of talking to do in your immediate future, remember? All the details."

Chandi smiled. "I remember, but it's kind of a long story and before I start, I should let you know I brought someone back with me from Oswego." Willem heard his cue and stepped into the doorway.

Lucy emitted even higher pitched sounds as she and Willem collided into each other. Chandi turned her head to give them a little privacy. When they finally broke from a long kiss, Willem picked up his bag in one hand and took Lucy's hand in the other. Lucy turned back into the room and hastily spoke to her roommate, "We'll talk later. Love you and glad you're not dead!" The pair took off down the hallway, leaving the door wide open.

Chandi laughed and started unpacking. There was a knock; Chandi turned around and saw Mika standing in her door. He rushed her and picked her up in his arms. "You're okay," he sighed. He was dusty and sweaty from a recent run; she breathed him in.

"Mika, I'm glad to see you, but I can't breathe," Chandi eked out.

He loosened his grip and Chandi's feet touched the floor. "I came as soon as the travel ban was lifted, but you weren't here. Lucy told me you had left and didn't know where you went," he explained.

"So you stopped by each night hoping to maul me?" Chandi teased him. Mika looked down sheepishly. She stepped on her tiptoes to give him a slightly less aggressive hug and then gave him a kiss on his cheek. "I'm glad to see you, too. Take a seat, I'm almost done unpacking." Chandi closed the door and moved her bag from her chair and onto the dresser. "So, Lucy's been catching you up?"

"Yup. I now know more about Willem Muller than I ever cared to," Mika jested as he took a seat.

"Did she also tell you I'm a tinker now?" Chandi asked, closing the bottom drawer with her foot and opening another.

"She retold the entire sordid tale of nanite infestation," he reported dramatically, eliciting a lyrical laugh from Chandi. "And she told me all about your quick thinking that let Willem go to Oswego temporarily."

Chandi did a mini-curtsy. "That was one of my finer moments."

He pulled her to the chair, and she sat sideways on his lap. He wrapped his arms around her and she relaxed into his embrace, unaware it was a set up. "She also told me how much you care about me and something about you making out with a merman, but that I shouldn't be worried because even if you were interested—which you weren't—his twig and berries aren't present when he's swimming." Chandi landed a few good jabs at his comment and she could feel Mika's laughter course through her body as he held her tight as a defensive maneuver.

After the playful tussle, she counted out on her fingers in her defense. "First, I didn't make out with anyone, he kissed me once and I turned him down once. Second, they all swim naked in Oswego and don't lie, you would have totally looked, too. How many mermen are you going to come across? Third, she was only suppose to tell you that if I didn't come back."

"So your plan was to only let me know how much you like me if you were missing or dead?" he teased her.

"Well…it sounds stupid when you say it," she replied.

He had an impish grin. "Is it so terrible that I know you care about me?"

Chandi moved her head from side to side. "No, but it complicates things." She watched the mirth leave his face and quickly tried to explain. "We're not married with a baby like Emma and Stephen. Or Willem and Lucy, who are so crazy about each other they would relocate to the shattered moon if it meant being together. I like spending time with you, and yes, I care about you. A lot. But you and I go where we are needed, and neither of us knows where that will take us. I just don't want to spend the time we have together trying to plan for the future because it may not lead us to the same place." Mika grew quiet and it made Chandi nervous. Hurting him was never her intent. "Say something?"

He posited a question, "Chandi, how many other tracers do you know that regularly come back to Unseen Waters between assignments?"

Chandi thought a moment. "Not many."

Mika shrugged. "And why would they? They know the drill. You come the Unseen Waters, you are going to be put to work. If you go to a regular church installation, they have lay staff and you have all the free time you want to do your own thing as long as you show up for morning devotion." He took hold of her hands. "What I'm saying is that the future isn't dictated to us. We make it through our choices. I choose to come back here, and that doesn't make me any less good of a tracer or boyfriend."

"Who said you were my boyfriend?" Chandi tried to sound stern, but her smile belied her delight with the term.

"The neutered merman you shot down." Mika smirked. "All I'm saying is it's okay for us to care about each other and still be who we are, as long as we are okay with it. We don't have to be like Lucy and Willem or Emma and Stephen, whoever they are. We are Chandi and Mika." He laced his fingers between hers.

"So we go where we are needed and when no one needs us, we go to each other?" Chandi spoke uncertainly.

Mika looked in her green eyes. "That's what I've been doing for months." He could see the realization sink in.

Chandi untangled her fingers and wrapped her arms

around his neck and pulled herself close to him, burrowing her head under his chin. He could feel her breath on the hairs of his neck. "Oh Mika…"

"Is that 'oh Mika, I'm such a fool to have not put that together sooner'? Or 'oh Mika, you don't need to keep coming back to Unseen Waters after this'?" He stayed still and waited for her answer.

"The first," she reassured him as she came up and gave him a soft kiss on the lips. "But I refuse to swoon for you."

He breathed easy and placed a flurry of soft kisses on her face and neck, causing Chandi to break out in giggles. "I can live with that."

A lascivious look crept onto Chandi's face. "When's the last time you had sex in a bunk bed?"

An ardent look entered his vulpine eyes. "Aren't you afraid Lucy will walk in on us?"

"I'll put a sock on the door. Plus, Willem's back…I probably won't see her until morning devotion." Chandi stroked up and down his arm and felt his bicep tighten.

Mika's hand caressed her thigh and hip as he hungrily kissed her. "Are you top or bottom?"

THE END